BITTERSWE

# BITTERSWEET HUMILIATION

## BY NICHOLAS P BOYLAND

This novel is a work of fiction and the characters and events in it exist only in its pages and in the author's imagination. They are not even distantly inspired by any individual or group known or unknown to the author. All incidents herein are pure invention.

All Rights Reserved including the right of reproduction in whole or in part in any form. This edition is published by Rhino Trikes. The text of this publication or any part thereof may not be reproduced or transmitted in any form or by any means, electronic or mechanical, including photocopying, recording, storage in an information retrieval system, or otherwise, without the written permission of the publisher.

This book is sold subject to the condition that it shall not, by way of trade or otherwise, be lent, resold, hired out, or otherwise circulated without the publisher's prior consent in any form of binding or cover other than that in which it is published and without a similar condition including this condition being imposed on the subsequent publisher.

The moral right of Nicholas P. Boyland has been asserted

First published in Great Britain 2013 by Rhino Trikes Church Street Winsham Nr Chard Somerset TA20 4JD

www.rhinotrikespublishing.com

## Published by Rhino Trikes

COPYRIGHT © NICHOLAS P. BOYLAND

ISBN 978-0-9576285-5-7

Cover photography by Kelly Boyland

Printed and bound in the UK by 4edge Limited

This book is dedicated to my dad Stanley Harold Roy Boyland

19.10.1928 – 13.06.2013

My inspiration - My number 1 fan - My friend

# PROLOGUE

## Farewell

Geoff Duckworth, 'Goose' to his friends, finished licking the glue on the envelope and sealed his final letter down.

He thought by putting the note under the covers of his mum's bed, somewhere it wouldn't be found immediately, his friends might receive the letters he'd sent them first. He hoped Mum wouldn't be the one to find him.

Geoff hadn't taken to civvy street well. In Germany, his skills had seen him seconded to 11SU, a signals unit working in the services' joint headquarters. As part of the Star Net detail he had a vital role monitoring 'Cold War' communications.

During the Falklands conflict, his 'special' role within the RAF had seen him involved in the 'Black Buck' missions. It had provided the penultimate achievement in his life; everything since had been disappointing. Sure, there was the brief but highly successful mission to rescue the daughter of his best friend's girlfriend from the hands of a deranged ex, but the higher the peaks, the deeper the troughs. Like so many former serviceman returning from the stress and excitement of a war zone, civvy street was just boredom and depression. Missing out on the recent Gulf war campaign had made Geoff feel that his life, or at least his usefulness, was over.

A detailed appraisal of Geoff's personal file by a qualified individual would probably identify all the hallmarks of a man suffering from Bi-Polar,

## Bittersweet Humiliation

Autism, or at the very least borderline personality disorder. It wasn't that he wanted to die; he just didn't want to continue to exist.

He stood upon the three legged table in the workshop and placed the meticulously wound 'marine grade' rope noose around his neck. Glancing up at the joist he had beefed up earlier, he double checked the integrity and suitability of the hook and bracket he'd made on the lathe. He wanted to make doubly sure that he didn't damage the roof joists. He couldn't bear to break things. Satisfied that all systems were in order, he prepared to tip the table up.

The peal of the phone intruded insistently into the workshop, though the heavy oak door muffled some of the sound both ways. Geoff cursed. He couldn't tolerate loose ends and a ringing phone would have to be answered before he could clock out.

He removed the noose from around his neck. The stool wobbled as he tried to step down, paralysing him with fear that he might fall and break a leg. Using the noose to steady himself he stepped down to the floor.

"Well, at least the noose would've held," he consoled himself.

He let himself back into the house and picked up the receiver.

"Goose, mate... it's Neil... I need your help."

"What's up Neil?" Geoff replied, acknowledging the gravity of Neil's tone.

"It's Brian, he's still alive!"

# CHAPTER ONE

**The honeymoon**

The hot Cretan sun streaked across the balcony, cutting through the blinds and illuminating the dancing dust particles, lighting the inside of the room with long luminescent streaks.

Natasha awoke with all the excitement of a little girl on holiday for the very first time.

"Neil," she wailed. "Come on, wakey wakey rise and shine there's a beautiful island out there to explore."

She jumped on the bed and straddled Neil's chest, dressed only in one of his shirts. "C'mon, c'mon Neil. I want to go out for breakfast. I want to go for a swim. I want some adventures."

Neil unbuttoned the loose flimsy shirt. "I know what adventure I want before anything else," he laughed. "Come here you."

"No Neil. Let's go and do something first, plenty of time for that later."

His hand was busy between her legs. She was still protesting she wanted to go out, but her pelvis was softly grinding back and forth, telling a different story.

Neil lifted her up by the buttocks. As his busy tongue went to work on her, the protests stopped abruptly, giving over to soft little moans. She slumped forward into the moment. Neil lifted her up. In one deft flowing movement he had her over, legs open, pinned down against the bed as he impaled her with his manhood. They made frantic, passionate love, abandoned in the moment, a million miles from the horror and torment waiting for them just around the corner.

Dressed in a tiny summer dress and strappy wedge sandals, wholly unsuitable for motorbike riding, Natasha danced out onto the patio where the little white bike was waiting. She pulled the smaller of the two helmets off the bars and popped it onto her head so that it sat just level with her ears; the bulk of it remained empty, hovering above her head like a huge alien brain.

Neil tapped the lid down playfully. The helmet squeezed over her ears, straps dropping into position below her chin.

"Ow!" she moaned, cuffing him playfully.

"Honestly, you've been like a schoolgirl since we got here," Neil commented.

"Killjoy!" she chastised, cuffing him again, then jumped on the back of the bike.

Neil threw his right leg over the bike and made himself comfortable on the front seat. His hands fell to Natasha's knees and he stroked his hands up her bare thighs, forcing her little dress upwards. "You naughty mare," Neil exclaimed, his hands arriving at the spot where her legs joined. "Haven't you forgotten something?"

Communicating with his reflection in the bike's mirrors, she put a finger to the corner of her mouth and said, "Ooooh, hmmm, what have I forgotten to put on?" Grabbing one of Neil's hands she placed it between her legs. "No, nothing down there forgotten."

He pulled his hand from her bare crotch, shook his head and started to ease the small helmet onto his big head. "You are such a diiirty cow!"

Natasha whacked the top of his helmet with her palm, causing his ear lobes to fold over.

"Ouch!" Neil exclaimed.

"That'll learn yuh! Less of the cow, boyfriend... Oops, I mean husband." She hugged him hard with arms and thighs. "Oooh, I do love the sound of that word... Husband. I never thought this moment would come."

"It'll be the last come you'll see if you whack me again, Knickerless Nickleby!" Neil warned.

"Come on Neil," she cooed. "I'm on my honeymoon. I want to be prepared at a moment's notice. See if I can't get you performing in nature. You know how I love a zipless fuck!"

"Hold on," Neil said as he kicked the little bike into life.

"Now you just drive carefully Mr Curland, remember, I didn't get my tetanus booster shot before we left, the doctor told me not to go stepping on any rusty nails!"

"Hold on tight!" Neil repeated.

"What?" Natasha questioned, leaning forward to hear him over the revvy little two stroke.

"Hold tight!" Neil repeated, grabbing her hands around his waist to emphasise.

Neil snicked the little bike into gear, revved the motor and dropped the clutch, hooking the front wheel into the air and taking off with an easy, well controlled wheelie.

"Wheeeeeeee!" Natasha squealed, her excitement levels right off the scale.

They rode for about twenty minutes, heading into the mountains, enjoying the waves of warm air buffeting their naked legs. Neil pulled off the road into the car park of a quaint little taverna on the side of the road.

"What are we stopping for?" Natasha asked.

"I noticed they have a map stand outside. We should buy a Greek map; all the place names on our tourist map are written in the Roman alphabet but a lot of the road signs are in bloody Cyrillic. I can't translate, but I can recognise the symbols. Having a 'native' map will make navigating the mountain roads easier."

Natasha touched her finger to the side of Neil's head and said, "OK Brains," in her very best 'Lady Penelope' voice from the 'Thunderbirds'.

"Oy you sarcastic bugger." Neil looked slightly hurt, insulted.

"No, I mean it," she reassured him. "You really are a clever guy. You make me feel so safe, so secure. You're my knight in shining armour and you always will be." She hugged him with real sincerity. "Now come on, let's ponder the map over a coffee for driver and a nice glass of red for moi."

They had spotted a spectacular natural attraction on the map, the 'Samaria Gorge'. Now according to the tourist guide there were two ways to visit the gorge. You could travel to the seaward side, take a boat to the mouth of the gorge, walk up to the very top, then catch a bus back down to the bottom and back to your vehicles. Alternatively, you could take a bus from Chania to the top of the gorge, walk down, and catch a boat to the bus park and a bus back to Chania. Or there was Neil and Natasha's way; find a remote village somewhere in the middle of a foreign country, at the top of a mountain, and head for that!

## CHAPTER TWO

**Fear of heights**

The mountain road wound round endlessly. Serpentine after serpentine. Neil was absolutely loving the ride. Only thing missing was the 1200 or so CCs which his Harley had over the little Yamaha. The fabulous weather and scenery made up for it though.

The tarmac came to an end but the road clearly continued on along a well-established dirt track. The little bike was equipped with spuddy tyres, so they pressed on.

A few miles along, they came to a narrow wooden bridge spanning easily one hundred feet of fissure. Neil stopped the bike on the nearside of the bridge and walked out on foot, checking if the bridge would support their weight. Despite the eight inch gaps between the planks, Neil was sure the bridge would support a small car. The drop to the floor of the valley was spectacular.

Natasha was frozen with fear. "Is this the gorge?"

"Nope, this is just a tributary. The gorge must be even more spectacular," he observed, looking at the map.

"I can't go over that Neil, I'm terrified of heights."

"Well it's not as high as the plane over here," Neil joked.

"I'm serious Neil. I can't do it," she answered, trembling.

## Bittersweet Humiliation

"Hey. I'm your knight in shining armour remember. Trust me, I promise you'll come to no harm."

"I can't Neil, I mean it!"

"I have an idea. Shut your eyes."

He took the helmet off her head, turned it around and fastened it on backwards.

"Hey," she shouted. "No funny!"

Before she could sort it out, Neil spun the little back wheel in the dust and powered across to the far side of the bridge.

"Neil, stop. You bastard! Not funny," she screamed.

"We're there," he sang, in an annoyingly squeaky voice.

"I'll never trust you again. I've got to worry about getting back over now," she moaned, pulling the annoying helmet off her head.

"Yea, but that's downhill, it'll be easier," he laughed.

"That's it," she teased, jumping off the stationary bike and lifting the front of her dress. "Fanny verbot." She used the German word Neil had taught her for 'forbidden' or 'off limits'.

"We'll see who lasts that one the longest," Neil gibed.

"Yea, you're right, it's my honeymoon. OK fanny verbot is suspended till we get home! Then you're really going to get it!"

"Oooh err. Ooh Missus… Promises promises," Neil joked in his very best Frankie Howard.

He took his helmet off, flicked the side stand down and put his arms around her.

"I love you Natasha. I've never loved anyone the way I love you. You make me laugh, you complete me!"

"Stop it you Muppet, you'll make me cry! I can't imagine ever being happier than I am now Neil."

"C'mon, let's go and find that gorge," Neil said, breaking the spell.

As they rounded the next bend, it became obvious that the dirt road only went as far as a deserted taverna.

They rode up to the main building. The place wasn't as deserted as it looked. Trade was not what you might call brisk though. Two gnarly old geezers sat under a threadbare Coca-Cola umbrella. A faded Coke mural adorned the facing wall of the building. A canned drinks fridge stood in the forecourt, the door hanging off by the remaining rusted hinge.

Natasha had jumped off the back of the bike, helmet on her elbow. Her long curls were blowing in the moderate mountain wind. The same breeze was causing her dress to blow flat against her chest, accentuating her ample curves, exaggerating the puffy swell of her nipples. The hem of the tiny dress was blowing, flapping in the cool breeze, leaving little to the imagination.

"Uh, Honey, I think it might be an idea if we don't stop here too long."

The men were staring at Natasha with looks of pure lust and disbelief on their faces.

"Uh Natasha, I really think we should head back now," Neil advised.

"Oh, but I'm thirsty. Why can't we stop for a drink?" She strode across to the two men, making a drinking gesture with her hand and saying, "Coca… Coca… Coca-Cola?"

Still staring in astonishment, one of the men put the hard-core porn magazine he was holding down onto the pile of porn scattered on the table top, and went to get up.

"No, no, it's OK we haven't time, we must go… So sorry, can't stop."

Natasha followed the men's stares to its logical conclusion, twigged the urgency in Neil's voice and followed his lead by hurrying back to the bike where they made a sharp exit stage left!

Natasha was starting to panic again as they approached the wooden bridge.

Just yards before the parapet, an angry looking dog leapt out of nowhere and lunged at her legs. She had to lift her legs up to avoid being savaged.

Neil gunned the motor; Natasha was still staring behind her making sure the attack had desisted. Before she knew it the bridge was behind them. Neil kept the motor cranked open until the engine spluttered to a halt a couple of miles on.

"Bugger," Neil exclaimed.

"What's up?"

"We're out of juice."

"How come?" she asked.

"Have you seen a petrol station up here? These things have only got small tanks."

"So what do we do now?" she asked, panicking, imagining mountain men charging after them in pick-up trucks.

"Well," Neil answered, "we still have the reserve tank. That might just get us from the foot of the mountain into Chania."

"How are we supposed to get down the mountain?" Natasha asked.

"We'll have to put gravity in the driving seat. Just like the crew of Apollo 13 did," Neil laughed. "Don't panic my fair maiden, didn't I tell you that downhill is easy?"

# CHAPTER THREE

**Merciless**

Brian Dix was lying on his back. The man sitting astride him was perhaps his size and half again. The fight had broken out over a stupid game of pool. Brian had been sitting close to the table and had refused to move when politely requested to do so by the huge Belfast man. The martial arts moves he had pulled were of little effect on the half inebriated man mountain. Besides getting a good hiding, Brian was in serious danger of looking a fool in front of the foot soldier who had been seconded to him.

On a small errand for his Provisional IRA handlers, he was unarmed, having left his usual armaments in the safe house in case of British army patrols. Things were not going swimmingly for him, and failure to resolve this quickly could see him in a world of shit.

His position alongside the Provisional IRA was tentative at best. He was not a soldier. Unlike most members, Brian was known to have no political commitment. His involvement with the Provo's began with his gun-running activities from Ireland to the mainland. His connections to the traveller community in the UK were a good source of revenue for the army, and Brian seemed willing to shoulder all the risks for the lean end of the rewards. To the Provo's, he was a mercenary with a death wish; an expendable commodity that could be extinguished the moment his usefulness expired.

## Bittersweet Humiliation

They had saved his arse at Cherry Tree Farm, that's for sure. That whole charade was staged to kill him off in the eyes of the Garda and the British authorities, that and to rub out a few of the paramilitary types he had been instructed to cosy up to. Thanks to outside interference it had turned deadly and he'd very nearly got killed in the crossfire.

*Bloody Neil Curland*, he thought. *How I'd like to get my hands on him!*

It wasn't often that someone got the drop on Brian Dix, and right now, focusing back on the immediate problem in hand, he was searching for a game changer, anything that could tip the scales in his favour.

It came when the man turned his head to see if his mates were backing him up.

As he turned back, Brian struck out with a thumb, jabbing it straight into the man's left eye with the force of a punch. Feeling the back of the socket, he ruthlessly gouged the eyeball out, leaving the organ hanging by the optic nerve and muscles, uselessly pointing down towards his naval.

Pain and shock rendered his opponent impotent.

Logically, Brian could easily have used the impasse as an opportunity to flee. The injured man could have been patched up, and Brian's anonymity, which had been won at Cherry Tree Farm for such a high price, would have been preserved and his mission saved. Brian Dix was not a great fan of logic.

As the man's hands involuntarily reached for the source of his pain, Brian's head shot forward like a coiled spring, head-butting his unfortunate opponent in the face and in so doing, removing any possibility of reversing the damage to his eye. Brian was easily able to throw the stunned man sideways and straddle him, pinning his arms beneath him and his body to the floor. The man's friends stood down, too shocked to take action.

"Look at me... Look at me," Brian shouted. Commanding the wounded man's full attention, he used his left thumb and forefinger to gouge out the man's right eye.

Brian Dix was back on the radar!

## CHAPTER FOUR

**Tempting fate**

Halfway down the mountain Neil spotted a small swing sign with writing on it; the sign was written in Greek alphabet but looked very similar to 'Benzine', the German word for petrol. Neil decided to give it a go and coasted into the drive.

The garage was just a lean-to connected to the side of a run-down cottage. Inside the garage was a series of forty-five gallon drums with hand cranking pumps inside them.

As the little bike skidded to a halt on the dusty drive, a wizened old man appeared from the depths of the garage. A fat, hand rolled cigarette was sticking out of the corner of his mouth. As he negotiated the numerous drums, a glowing blim of tobacco and ash, the bulk of his smoke, dropped out and landed on the drums of high octane fuel. He cursed and poked a stained stubby finger onto the glow to render it impotent.

"Benzina? Benzine?" Neil questioned, impatient, not wanting to linger in the deathtrap longer than necessary.

The old man, ignoring the heavy petrol fumes, was distracted, trying to get his stubborn dog end to re-light with a Bic lighter.

Neil repeated the request, "Benzina? Benzine? Petrol? Gasolina?" gesturing towards the fuel tank.

The old man gave up trying to light his lower lip and answered, "Benzine? Nai." He started furiously cranking the handle of one of the pumps, priming it up.

## Bittersweet Humiliation

Neil opened the petrol tank of the bike as the old man opened the valve on the nozzle, letting the fluid flow into the tank.

Natasha had spotted a wild orange grove inside an ancient graveyard opposite and had rushed off to investigate, camera in hand.

Neil concluded the business and paid the man before pushing the bike a safe distance away, then joined Natasha to see what had caught her attention.

Climbing on top of an ancient grass covered crypt, she was at full stretch reaching for the biggest, most juicy looking orange in the grove.

"Should you be up there?" he called out.

"Not doing any harm, they're just growing wild," she replied.

"No, I meant, should you be climbing on top of a crypt? It's a bit disrespectful; they might get funny about that sort of thing around here."

"Crypt?" she questioned in a terse whisper. "I thought it was a shed." Panicking, she jumped down, landing with a tortured squeal. "Owww! Neil!"

She slumped to a squatting position, hands instinctively cradling her foot, obviously in pain.

"What? What have you done you silly mare?"

"I've stepped on a wasp or something." She was really crying now.

"Let go of your foot. Let me have a look. Let me see."

Neil gently turned her foot over. Stuck to the bottom of her sandal was a piece of old pallet. Through the pallet was a rusty old nail, which was now sticking through pallet, sandal and some way into the ball of Natasha's foot.

He gently stroked his thumb over the top of Natasha's foot, gauging how far into it the nail had travelled. Convinced that it was not all the way in, he decided to yank it out before she knew what he was doing.

"Ouch, ow, ow, owwww," she screamed as Neil whipped out the offending article.

The wound was not serious, but it would likely bruise up and become very painful to walk on for a bit.

"What was it? How's it look?" she whimpered.

"Oh it's nothing," he replied. "Just a little tack. Nothing dramatic. No blood at all. Now just you man up. Your sandal's hurt worse than you are."

The nail was frighteningly long. Luckily, it had gone in at an angle, with the wedge of the sandal absorbing much of the length. Nevertheless, a good inch of fat rusty nail had punctured flesh and muscle of her foot.

Natasha slapped him. "A little sympathy please!"

"C'mon, we'll get on down to Chania, get you some iodine and a plaster, then we'll get on back to Kalyves."

Neil fired up the little bike. Natasha hobbled over and with animated effort gingerly threw her injured foot over the saddle, wincing as her foot contacted the foot-peg.

"Get over yourself, you drama queen," Neil scoffed, receiving another cuff around the ears for his cheek!

"Oy!" he complained. "Quit that before I forget I'm a gentleman!"

"A gentleman would be more sympathetic, you're no gentleman Curland, you're nothing but a brute. I'm seriously injured and you just don't care. I don't even know why I married you."

"Get that out of my neck," Neil complained. "I can't ride the bike with *that* sticking in the back of my neck!"

"With what sticking in the back of your neck? There's *nothing* sticking in your neck," she squealed.

"Your bottom lip, it's jabbing me in the neck!"

With that, they sped off down the road, leaving Natasha's complaints lost to the wind.

The ride back down the mountain was a hoot. Neil was messing around, trying to grope Natasha with his left hand and she, in turn, was slapping him as hard as she could without endangering the bike's stability.

As they reached the foothills, the signs of civilisation returned. With increasing regularity they found themselves passing tradesmen and houses on the side of the road, with the occupants engaging in the daily al-fresco living common in hot countries. Neil checked his errant behaviour and stopped trying to fondle his wife's breasts.

A long line of cars following a slow tractor caused him to brake sharply. Directly opposite was a shanty-stall selling tourist shizzle and fresh fruit. A coach party of tourists, obviously football supporters from the football shirts and scarves hanging in the windows, had pulled over and the stall was doing brisk trade.

Her injured foot temporarily forgotten, Natasha had a wicked thought of how to get her own back on Neil and have a little fun into the bargain.

Leaning forward, she slipped Neil's wallet out of his pocket and hopped off the back of the bike.

Taking her helmet off, she plonked it over the mirror, then, careful not to put weight on her injured foot, she limped across to the stall and picked up a bag of cherries. Taking two cherries from the bag she turned towards Neil, turning away from the stall as she did. With exaggerated posturing, akin to a magician's assistant, she slipped the straps of her summer dress down off her shoulders. Popping the cherries down her front and pulling the straps back up, she strolled over to the vendor to pay for her purchase. The fruit down her dress, coupled with slightly more than a generous handful of nature's bounty, had the view from the front looking quite obscene. The football fans were cheering and wolf-whistling fit to burst.

Natasha was playing to the crowd, striking poses like a fashion model. Neil decided enough was enough.

"OK, you win, I'm sorry. Now c'mon, let's get out of here before you cause a riot," Neil said, shaking his head.

Hopping back on the bike, Natasha had one last surprise in store for Neil and a farewell treat for her admirers. Dropping both the straps on her dress she expelled the cherries, exposing her breasts to the admiring glances of the coach party. A cheer went up as the lads enjoyed the impromptu 'flash'.

Neil shook his head in a gesture of disapproval as the revving engine drowned out Natasha's mocking laughter!

## CHAPTER FIVE

### Old habits

The pharmacist advised Natasha to see the doctor for a tetanus booster. She assured him that her jabs were up to date, so he sent her on with an antiseptic tincture.

Neil, engrossed in browsing the fake Oakley sunglasses, looked up and asked, "Well?"

"Oh, nothing, he's given me some antiseptic cream, he says it's fine," she lied.

Neil was struggling to decide between a pair of aviators and a pair of biker style 'wrap-arounds'. "Which d'you reckon?" he asked.

"Neil," she chastised, then in a hoarse whisper added, "Neil Curland, you're a very wealthy man, why on earth do you want fake sunglasses? They'll damage your eyesight!"

Neil smiled, put the glasses back and remarked, "Old habits I suppose. I still can't resist a bargain."

Back in the familiar surroundings of Kalyves, Neil and Natasha parked the bike up and prepared for an evening out in the resort, which was a comfortable stroll from their accommodation.

Natasha bravely donned a pair of stiletto sandals, determined to look drop dead sexy, despite the discomfort of her injured foot.

They found a taverna along the beach front, and were quickly seated close to the water's edge.

"Red wine?" Neil asked, preparing to order drinks for the evening.

## Bittersweet Humiliation

"Yes please," Natasha replied.

With few paying customers to serve in this late part of the holiday season, the waiter quickly arrived at the table.

Neil was in the process of ordering a bottle of house red when Natasha stopped him.

"Just a glass Neil, I don't really fancy a bottle," she said.

Neil raised an eyebrow questioningly; Natasha was no alcoholic, but she would normally consume a bottle to herself on a night out.

"I've taken painkillers for my foot and they're making me a little light headed," she replied to his unasked question.

"OK. Just a glass of house red, and a dark rum and Coke please," he requested of the waiter who, of course, spoke English fluently.

Natasha was reluctant to drink too much because of the possibility that she might be pregnant, but she didn't want Neil suspecting that something might be up. Besides, she had not been instructed to abstain from alcohol completely during any of her pregnancies. Everything in moderation was the buzzword of the day!

Keen to enjoy their holiday to the full, Neil, ignorant of her noble reasons for restraint, was urging her to join him in their first holiday blow-out. The red wine continued to flow. Natasha was foolishly using Neil's infrequent visits to the loo as an opportunity to tip the contents of her glass onto the sand. Unfortunately, her more numerous visits to the little girl's room seemed to result in her glass miraculously refilling.

It was in this way that she lost count of how many she had consumed, and she began to feel the effects of the alcohol, her resolve giving way to the tempting voice in her head telling her that the pregnancy was as yet unconfirmed and probably a false alarm. Eventually, the battle was lost and the inebriated couple found themselves swaying along the beach in high spirits.

As Natasha sashayed along the water's edge, the cool breeze gently rippling the water's surface flattened the thin material of her Indian cotton dress against the subtle curves of her sensuous body. In the silver light from the full moon, Neil was captivated by the way her sensual nipples disturbed the fabric of her dress, as the natural choreography of her hips caused her breasts to rise and fall with the motion of her steps. Spontaneously, a playful Natasha broke into a run towards the surf. By the time she splashed her first steps into the cool inviting briny her dress was off, thrown haphazardly onto the wet sand.

"C'mon Neil," she shouted. "Come swim with me."

Neil watched bewitched as her beautiful naked form slipped elegantly into the waves. In response to the enchanting spectacle of this naked water nymph, he clumsily attempted to relieve his own body of the encumbrance of clothing. Every move Natasha made was with the relaxed sexuality of a Prima Ballerina. Neil, in contrast, was as elegant as a rugby player in Dr Marten boots!

He swam out to join her. She was just out of her depth. He, in contrast, could still touch the bottom with his feet flat.

She hugged her arms around his neck, wrapping her legs around his waist.

"Make love to me Neil," she whispered huskily in his ear.

Despite his inherent clumsiness, Neil's body was in tune with Natasha's needs and in a fluid movement the two were joined. They combined slowly, gently, enjoying the ebb and flow of the liquid supporting them, connecting them. The current gently encouraged them into the shallows, eventually depositing them on the sand in a seamless transfer.

"Neil, I'm getting sand inside my 'you know what', it's a little bit uncomfortable," Natasha softly whimpered.

The swirling waters of the shallows were indeed depositing grains of sand in undesirable places.

"Can we move a little further up the beach, onto the dry sand?" she asked, keeping the tone an aroused whisper, keen not to spoil the mood.

Straight up the beach from the water's edge was a small boat. Little more than a rowing boat, it presented the perfect place to continue their romantic liaison away from the infernal sand. Natasha lay back in the shallow hull of the little boat, her legs open, inviting. Neil was quickly back up to strength and entered her with the same enthusiasm he had shown earlier.

"What was that?" he enquired suddenly, disturbed.

"Don't stop," Natasha begged.

"Someone's there," Neil announced, startled, his ardour waning slightly.

"Please, don't stop Neil," Natasha reiterated.

Now, Neil focused with clarity upon the man lying on a blanket stretched out on the sand between the boat and its nearest neighbour.

"Natasha, there's a guy lying next to us, not six foot away, he's staring at us."

Natasha looked towards where Neil was gesturing. There was indeed a gentleman reclining on the sand and he was propped on one elbow, staring straight at them.

Natasha stared at Neil, her nostrils flaring in that manner which told him that she was powerfully turned on!

"Don't stop Neil," she growled. "Don't you dare stop!"

The expression on her face was clearly visible to him in the bright moonlight. That look never failed to send floods of testosterone into Neil's bloodstream. He returned to the task with renewed vigour.

Out of the corner of his eye, Neil could see that the man had moved closer. He could see that he had gone from passive voyeur to actively participating, albeit without any physical contact with the couple.

Natasha's passionate moans were indicative of her obvious enjoyment at being the centre of attention; she couldn't take her eyes off what her appreciative watcher was doing to himself.

"Fuck me Neil, oh, fuck me harder," she cried, her enthusiasm dispelling any reservations Neil may have had.

They arrived at a noisy, passionate orgasm pretty much simultaneously. Neil was on his knees in the hull of the dinghy with Natasha laid on the centre bench, her torso supported by an assortment of buoys and inflatables in the front of the sloop.

Within seconds of Neil's body convulsing rigidly, pumping his seed deep within her pliant body, the voyeur too arrived at his climax, pumping his own expression of gratitude over Natasha's heaving bosom.

"What the hell just happened?" Neil questioned as their uninvited guest grabbed his blanket and departed rapidly into the night.

Retrieving their discarded clothing from the beach, Neil turned to Natasha, confused.

"I thought we weren't going to play these games anymore?" Neil said, gravely. "Remember where it went before? I don't want that again!"

Natasha sensed the tension in his voice and took his face in her hands.

"I love you Neil. I love you with all my heart. We both know that we have kinky, naughty tendencies and I, for one, love it. We're unpredictable Neil. Our lovemaking is wild and exciting. We know the boundaries now because we've been beyond them. I only ever want to be with you, and I will never, ever again let another man do to me what you do. That, I promise," she laughed. "But I make you another promise; I'll never let you get bored with me!"

"That's a relief," he laughed, hugging her into a tight embrace. "As long as you know I will never share you again, anything else goes." He added, "I must admit though, I do love your kinky side. You keep me on my toes!"

"That's the plan lover," she laughed, and pulled free of him, breaking into a trot up the beach. "C'mon, let's get back to our room and do it again!"

Neil burst out laughing and ran after her.

## CHAPTER SIX

**Bless**

It wasn't long before the end of the fortnight break came around. The opportunity for the two of them to spend time together, without children, and without outside interference was like a tonic; full of cathartic goodness. It was a reluctant, slightly saddened Neil who parted with the little bike on the final day of their honeymoon.

"We've certainly had some fun on that thing," Neil remarked as the bike was loaded into the back of the hire company van. "Back to the grindstone I suppose?"

"You don't have to go back to work you know Neil," Natasha remarked. "There's no need for us to take on the world. We have a good income, my investments are doing OK. You said yourself that your business can survive without you now. There's nothing stopping us from holidaying on as long as we like, not really."

"Oh, I'd get bored if I didn't work, I'm hardwired for it! Onwards and upwards I guess. It would be nice to stay away a little longer though."

Natasha smiled inwardly to herself.

Most of the holidaymakers the couple had arrived with a fortnight ago were noisily bustling around the hotel reception. Natasha explained to the rep that they would not be joining the coach for the trip to the airport.

"What gives Natasha? How come we're not flying from Heraklion?"

"We have a taxi booked Neil, our flight departs from Chania; we're flying to Madrid."

"If you have an explanation tucked away up your sleeve darling, I think this would be a good time to deploy it," Neil said with a touch of impatience in his voice.

"Neil, I have a little surprise for you," Natasha confessed.

"Should I be delighted or frightened?" Neil questioned.

"We're not flying home Neil, we're flying over to Warren's ranch."

"What about the kids?"

"They're already there Neil. Warren and Nell flew over yesterday and picked them up." She smiled a little smug smile. "They should get there a few hours before we do."

"You devious mare," Neil playfully chastised. "What about work?"

"Oh Neil, honestly, you have more work to do over in the States than you do back home right now. Warren has offered to organise a whole raft of social meetings for you with network moguls and the like." Her eyes narrowed slightly. "Besides, I have another surprise in store."

"Oh dear," Neil exclaimed. "Not sure I like the sound of this."

"Warren is throwing us a lavish blessing," she giggled.

"What, you're joking? We just *got* married."

"Oh don't be a spoilsport Neil, Warren wanted to be a part of our nuptials, but knew our wedding would've become a media circus. This was an ideal compromise. If Warren couldn't come to the wedding, the wedding can come to him!"

"I don't think I'll ever get used to being wealthy."

Natasha hugged him to her. "Oh Neil, it will be wonderful, just you wait and see."

Organised through Warren, the flights were business class all the way. Neil was still struggling to come to terms with moving in wealthy circles.

"Don't know why we have to travel in such vulgar opulence," he complained. "We'd still have arrived at the same time if we'd travelled steerage and spent a fraction of the money."

"Yes, and we'd be cooped up like battery hens. You'd be sitting with your knees sticking in your ears, with some fat German kid kicking you in the back and I'd have some drunk Scottish bloke leering down my top, belching fag breath and half-digested burger in my face. Besides, we're wealthy, we have a duty to travel business class, it subsidises the ticket price of those less fortunate than ourselves," Natasha concluded.

"Let them eat cake," Neil quoted, with sarcastic wit. "You, my dear Queen Natasha Antoinette, will be first against the wall, come the revolution."

"Oh well, I like having money Neil, if you want me to feel guilty about it you can go to hell," she retaliated.

Neil laughed and threw an arm around her shoulders. "You're right, of course, and I *would* hate the knees in my ears thing. I would sort out the fat German kid though."

"Oh?"

"I'd pick him up by his lederhosen and shove the little bastard in the overhead locker. Shove a couple of tins of knockwursts in there with him, that would keep him occupied all night," Neil laughed.

"Oooh, that's a cruel stereotype. It is true though isn't it? German kids seem so unruly when they're on holiday," Natasha said.

"Mmm, they aren't especially different to our children," Neil explained. "They are perhaps a lot more disciplined than kids in the UK. They have an incredibly strong, ingrained work ethic. They go to school really early in the morning and I think in general they're worked a lot harder. The parents are not big on corporal punishment though."

Natasha's eyes glazed over a bit as she realised she had inadvertently started Neil on one of his *when I lived in Germany* stories.

"Reminds me of an amusing story though," Neil began. "One that actually happened. It's a bit of an urban legend now, but I was there and can vouch for its authenticity."

The plane had started its taxi run towards the end of the runway for take-off. This was the bit Natasha was most terrified of. She encouraged Neil to continue.

"Well, we were Christmas shopping, me and the girlfriend of the time. Stood in the queue at the checkouts, along with a whole line of other pissed off shoppers. We were dressed for the Arctic conditions outside, despite the thermostat in the shop being nailed in the red." He hesitated, making sure no-one else within earshot was listening. "Well, just behind us was this dumpy little squaddie wife, a screaming brat in the trolley, one in her belly furiously kicking. Her husband probably on an unaccompanied posting, stationed in Northern Ireland or somewhere overseas. She had another little toe rag doing his damnedest to lose his mum's hand, and redirect all the tempting candy on display into mum's trolley. Now all at once, it becomes too much for our forced single mum and after repeated warnings, she slaps the errant youngster squarely on the arse, which has the desired effect and stuns him into silence." Neil paused again to make sure he still had Natasha's undivided attention.

"Go on!" she whispered.

"With the same, this big, well dressed, hoity toity type behind her pipes up, in indignant, broken English announcing, *Hin Germany, ve do not hit our children!* Without a moment's hesitation, little squaddie wife retaliates with, *In England, we do not gas our Jews.*" Neil took a deep breath. "The woman was speechless. Honestly, I didn't know whether to laugh or cry. I've never left a shop so quickly in my life. True story!"

Just then the punch line was forgotten as the engines were throttled to full speed and the jet was catapulted down the runway towards take off!

Natasha grabbed hold of Neil's hand and squeezed until the circulation in his fingers stopped.

"Do you have a little story about the leering Scotsman?" Neil asked, in an attempt to distract her.

After a change in Madrid and an unremarkable overnight flight, they arrived in Fort Worth, where a limousine was waiting to carry them onto Marble Falls and the lavish comfort of the Bateson Ranch.

## CHAPTER SEVEN

### Toe the line

Brian and his cohort escaped the bar with the skin of their teeth. All hell broke loose when the shock and awe of his frenzied attack had subsided and the regulars realised that a friend of theirs had just been permanently mutilated.

He had to abort the mission and hot-tail it back to the safe house. His IRA puppeteers were getting mighty sick of Brian's temper which so often of late had led to him screwing up. He knew that he was out on a limb with his superiors, and would need to show some loyalty and dedication in future if he were to avoid taking a short trip out on a country road at the dead of night.

Back in the south, he had a number of business ventures on the go, backed by his masters; lucrative brothels, staffed by young girls, mostly Slavic, from the Russian Far East, girls who had ventured over seeking a better life. Instead of a better life, they encountered men like Brian, who had them addicted to hard drugs and working on their backs within weeks of arriving. He was a good whoremaster, and it was the bountiful earnings from these ventures that kept the volatile Brian from becoming just another casualty of war.

It was the other ventures on the side that would compromise him. The ones he kept a secret from his IRA bosses. Since the run in with Neil Curland raised his profile and brought him under the scrutiny of the authorities, Brian relied on his IRA masters to ensure his continued liberty, health and wealth. They made sure he had enough of each commodity to keep him loyal, but not enough for him to get above his station. The conspicuousness of wealth was something, under such conditions, Brian could not entertain. His trickle of clandestine operations, kept well below the radar, supplied him with the personal funds he needed, were the opportunity to ever arise, for him to break away, disappear, and start a new life.

## CHAPTER EIGHT

**Fore!**

"Do you play golf Neil?" Warren asked.

"I have been known to visit the driving range once in a while, if I can find the time."

"A man needs a hobby. It stops itchy feet syndrome," Warren replied.

"I remember one time," Neil reminisced, "I played against a golf-mad friend, played the entire round with a nine iron, it was the only club I possessed."

"You're going to tell me you played an under par game and thrashed your friend?" Warren suggested, one eyebrow raised.

"No, as it happens," he laughed. "I seem to remember I got thrown off the course for lying down on the green, using my nine iron as a snooker cue." He added, "I used to bore easily."

"It's not really a young man's sport," Warren agreed. "I'll just go and set the girls up with their horses, and then you and I can tee off. You'll find my course quite interesting."

"18 hole?" Neil enquired.

"Of course. You'll love it Neil, I've got a couple of fairways where you have to drive clean across a lake to reach the green. Separates the men from the boys."

## CHAPTER NINE

### One size fits all

Warren's wife, Nell, was at the stables with Natasha and the children as Neil and Warren approached.

"Monica is a little young to ride on her own. I will just walk her round the paddock I think," Natasha suggested sensibly.

"Oh don't you be worrying girl. She'll be fine," Warren reassured her.

"She's a bit small to be perched way up on a pony," Natasha protested.

"If I tell you a hen dips snuff, you can look under her wing," Warren offered.

Natasha raised an enquiring eyebrow.

"I hope to be kicked to death by grasshoppers if I ain't telling the truth," Warren offered as an explanation.

He opened the door to a seemingly empty stable, but inside stood a pony. It was no taller than Monica.

Warren laughed. "See, you can't tell how deep a well is by measuring the length of the pump handle."

"You're a card Warren," Natasha laughed, hugging the huge Texan.

"We bought us a couple of Welsh Cobs for our girls when they were young. Damned if I knew the things could live so long."

"How old are they?" Natasha enquired, concerned.

"Oh, don't you worry, they're in their prime, about 15 years old. They'll live to 25-30 years old," he grinned. "We'll have the damn things around for a few years to come yet. I haven't the heart to let them go, they're part of the family."

Monica was fascinated by the tiny little ponies.

"Shall I take David with me or will he be OK with you girls?" Neil asked.

Little David was doing his damnedest to climb aboard one of the docile little animals, by clinging to its mane and swinging back and forth. He'd made his choice.

"I think he'll be OK with us," Natasha laughed, as Nell started to tack up the ponies.

With a cacophony of whoops and screeches the happy little pony train wobbled its way from the paddock and out towards the open range.

Warren buzzed through the intercom to the main house. Within a matter of minutes, a pair of immaculately dressed caddies in golf carts appeared. "We'll manage ourselves, thank you Greg, you boys can go and make yourselves comfortable for a few hours," he said to the older of the two. "I'll call you if we need anything." He gestured to the two way radio he had in his shoulder bag.

The two men nodded and started back in the direction of the main ranch house.

"Greg," Warren called out, "pop both the bags into one cart, you boys can take the second cart on back to the house, we'll manage with just the one."

As they reached the first tee box, Warren questioned, "Honours?"

"Oh no, no need, you tee off Warren. I'll be trailing after the first hole anyway, for sure."

"Neil, there's something I need to ask you. You seem like a stand up sort of guy, so I can't get an angle on why you and Natasha ended up so far off the rails? I just don't get it, you're not a player but what you were doing was somehow worse. You can tell me to butt out if you like but it would sure help me to understand you, if I could hear your side."

Despite the embarrassment of the question, Neil felt Warren's loyalty and support for Natasha warranted some sort of explanation.

After a contemplative pause, Neil offered, "I wish I could explain things Warren, but I can't. I have no explanation for what happened, or why. I have tried to make sense of things in my own mind, but all I can really offer is that we let our fantasies become a reality. I have nothing but regrets about that period of our lives. Needless to say it's over, history, just a bad memory. We have the rest of our lives now to replace the hurt with new experiences, good memories. I promise you, I will spend the rest of my life making up for my past mistakes and Natasha feels the same."

"Well Neil, that kinda puts my mind at rest. I've had a hard time connecting the guy that Natasha has been raving about for the past year with the things she's told me about her past life. Speaking to the two of you, I think you're both missing something in your lives, maybe something the good book could help you with." Seeing Neil's eyes involuntarily roll, Warren hastened to add, "Oh don't worry Neil, I'm not about to get preachy on you. God knows the good book has helped me out of a few sticky situations, but I don't believe it can help you unless you invite it in to your life, that's for you to work out for yourselves.

Perhaps you could indulge an old man and just keep an open mind to it?"

"Well Warren, it would take an epiphany to get me to turn to the Bible, but that said, if I was served with a burning bush, I wouldn't deny it."

"That's good enough for me son; open mind, open heart. Now c'mon, let's get this round started."

## CHAPTER TEN

**Divinity**

Warren Bateson's property was vast. He had an expanse of prairie, woodland, a small but picturesque waterfall cascading from the granite hill, and an area of lakeside, all as his back yard. Most of the property was protected, surrounded as it was by the natural boundaries of the Colorado River and the hills and lake. The buildings and golf course were, however, securely fenced. A necessary precaution for any celebrity in these fame obsessed times.

To the west of the property was the Bateson's own chapel, which they enjoyed as a Sunday ritual, the family being devout Methodists. This was a topic of interest with Neil; although himself an Atheist, his family were Methodists and it was in this denomination that he had been christened, something which seemed to please Warren greatly.

The private chapel was to play host to the blessing of Neil and Natasha's wedding. First, there was something which Warren had to clear up with the happy couple.

"Neil, I know you're not a religious man, and Natasha, I know that you are technically of a Catholic persuasion."

"Not really Warren," Natasha interrupted. "My dad was Catholic, so I took baptism, confirmation and communion, but to be fair, after dad died and we left Italy, I haven't been back to mass or anything. I'm just a Christian now, but unlike my *husband*," she poked Neil in the arm, "I do believe in God and in his son, Jesus Christ. I loved my dad and my nan and granddad and I know I will see them again someday." Neil inwardly grimaced, but said nothing.

"Well," Warren continued, "I just wanted to say that we, me and Nell, would be mighty proud and gratified if you two would attend a service with us on Sunday, just so's we can introduce you to the Reverend, and touch base with God, before we ask him, formal like, to bless your holy union and all." Warren was clearly a little embarrassed, thinking this was perhaps a big ask for someone like Neil who had publicly stated his atheist beliefs.

"Warren," Neil replied, "we," he turned to Natasha and held her hand, "and I am sure I speak for us both now, we would be honoured to join you for service. I'm sure that your God won't be offended by me speaking to him and asking for his blessing."

Warren's face broke into a warm infectious smile. "That's mighty fine Neil, mighty fine. If I felt any better, I'd drop my harp plumb through the cloud."

The Sunday service was really quite enjoyable. Without the pretentious crowd of pious church goers, the service seemed to have far more meaning, more significance. Watching the children humming along to the hymns, even the stoic Neil found himself singing and praying without the usual reserve he felt at weddings and funerals. Although not about to embrace God, he couldn't help but feel a little warm and fuzzy, sharing this experience with the people he loved and close friends. For once, in this situation, he didn't feel like a fraud.

"Well Neil, wasn't so awful was it?" Warren asked.

"Not at all Warren," Neil replied. "Not at all."

The following week saw Nell and Natasha make the final preparations for the blessing. It would be a very private affair, just Warren's family, Neil, Natasha, the children and the good Reverend. As far as Neil was aware, after the service there would be a small gathering of a few of Warren's celebrity and influential friends; just a few names that Natasha had expressed a wish to meet, plus a few invited heads that would hold influence over Neil's future venture. At least, that was what he was led to believe.

## CHAPTER ELEVEN

**Ones and noughts**

While the girls were busy with the blessing arrangements, Neil and Warren flew out to Beverly Hills on a little 'meet and greet' mission with heads of networks and studios. Warren certainly had the key to the door in Hollywood.

Back in their hotel suite, Warren poured a couple of shots of bourbon for himself and Neil. "I've taken the liberty of inviting a couple of guys over for you to meet Neil. They're not movers and shakers; you won't have to charm them. They're a couple of independents, straight out of Caltech. It occurs to me that with your experience building stage props, there may be some crossover work into what they're about."

Neil raised an eyebrow. "What is it that they're about?"

"Well Neil, to tell you the truth, it's all a bit over my head, but my good friend and financial adviser, Harvey Goldstein, tells me it's something I want to get involved with."

"Can you give me a clue?"

"Well now, I'm sure you know how cartoons work, with drawings and a Rostrum camera?"

"Yes I do Warren. In fact, a good friend of mine is a Rostrum cameraman with the BBC back home."

"Good, good. See I knew this would be up your street. Well these two whizz kids it seems are some sort of computer boffins. They've formed their own company, 'Fizzy Door Productions'. What these guys are into is CGI."

## Bittersweet Humiliation

Neil butted in, "Computer generated imagery."

"That's right Neil, computer generated graphics. To be more specific, they concentrate on film stunt work, carried out through graphics, generated on a computer. They're way ahead of the field by all accounts."

"How can I help?" Neil asked.

"Just have a chat with the guys, get a feel for what they're about. You build props for the movie industry; see if there is any crossover between what you do and what they do. Mainly Neil, I want you to form an opinion, advise me how deep you think I should go. The guys need funding see; I think that's where I come in."

The meeting was a pleasant one. Neil was highly impressed by the knowledge and enthusiasm the guys showed. Warren was not highly impressed by their attire, but Neil assured him this was typical of men who worked with their brains rather than their smiles. All in all, Neil couldn't really see any angle for him in their work as it was all with scale models and blue screen technology. He knew a few people in the micro engineering and animatronics world back home in the UK that would be interested, but that was as far as it went.

"It's definitely an industry with a future Warren, and if anyone can make a go of it I reckon those two can. I might even invest a few bob with you. I can see a time when studios won't need to pay me to build props; they'll just create them on the computer."

"Thanks Neil, I appreciate your advice. I'm thinking I might just have a flutter on them."

## CHAPTER TWELVE

**Surprise**

Warren was really spoiling his new found friend. After touching down on the tarmac at Fort Worth, they were whisked off by limousine to a waiting helicopter, which flew them directly back to the helipad at the ranch in Marble Falls, where preparation for the blessing was in full swing.

Neil was forbidden from seeing his bride until the ceremony.

"We're under starters orders now Neil. The girls are running the show. How does it feel?" Warren asked.

"Honestly Warren? I feel a bit of a fraud. I've only just done the romantic wedding bit. I appreciate that you weren't able to attend, and I fully understand how you didn't want your appearance to upstage Natasha's big day. I just hope it's not too much of a Disney wedding. I'm a bit of a wallflower on the sly. Still, it's all for Natasha, and whatever makes her happy will make me happy."

"That's the spirit Neil. You've got a 'one in a million' girl there; rich, gorgeous, clever and humble too. Those are rare commodities in an attractive woman, I can tell you."

"Well, I did kiss a fair few frogs before I found my princess, Warren, that's for sure. You must have known a few divas in your time, I'll dare say?"

"You're not wrong there Neil, my business is full of 'em. Fortunately for me, I married my childhood sweetheart, so I've always had immunity from all that nonsense. I sure have seen some powerful men fall under the wiles of a shrew."

"You are charmingly old fashioned Warren," Neil laughed.

That night, Neil slept alone. He would face tomorrow with equal helpings of anticipation and trepidation. The day was in Natasha's hands. He only hoped it wouldn't be too Hollywood.

Neil was sleeping soundly when Warren burst into his quarters, brandishing a tray containing steaming hot coffee and a bowl of grits.

"C'mon buddy, rise and shine, time to get married again!"

"The condemned man pleads not guilty your honour. It wasn't me, a big boy did it and ran away," Neil groaned.

"C'mon Neil, it's not every day you get to marry a gorgeous gal twice!"

Breakfast dispensed with, dressed in dressing gowns, the men retired to their respective bathrooms and emerged dressed in casuals.

Warren had organised a trim and spruce up from his studio hairdresser for the two men, after which they donned their suits, chosen for them by the women.

"Look at you, you old spiv," Neil joked.

"What the hell is a spiv?" Warren replied, puzzled.

"You look stoating Warren, proper dapper."

"Do me a favour Neil, do I look OK or not? I can't follow your English phrases."

"Warren, you look… cool. Is that international enough for you?"

Warren looked in the mirror.

"Goddamn it! If you ask me, I look like I've been chewed up, spit out, and stepped on!"

Neil laughed out loud.

"Warren, if I was nervous before, I'm not now! Your comedic timing is spot on, you missed your calling. You should have gone into stand up."

Joking aside, both men were actually quite pleased with the modest double breasted dark suits Natasha had chosen. Thanks to Warren's expensive tailor, the outfits fitted perfectly.

Standing at the altar again so soon Neil was feeling a little self-conscious. He was looking forward to seeing Natasha once again in a beautiful wedding gown, but was slightly disappointed that, this time, he wouldn't be surrounded by his best friends and loved ones. Warren was at his side standing in as the best man. As the first bars of the wedding march drifted through the tiny chapel, Neil turned to face the door, waiting in anticipation of the bride's arrival. There was some sort of commotion outside the door.

"I'll just go and find out what the hold-up is Neil. Stay here, I'll be back in one half less than no time." With that, Warren went off to investigate.

Neil was slightly puzzled when Warren reappeared in the ornate, hand carved doorway, accompanying his bride on her left, deputising for her deceased father.

A cough to Neil's right convinced him to turn to see who was standing there in the position so recently vacated by Warren. Natasha had surpassed herself. Completely behind Neil's back, and without his knowledge, she had organised for his elder brother John to be the best man for the blessing.

"Jesus Christ John," Neil exclaimed.

"Steady on old chap," his brother cautioned. "God's house and all that."

"Hell John, you're a sight for sore eyes."

The two men embraced and the tears welled up in both their eyes.

They hadn't seen each other in years. Once really close, John had married an Australian woman while Neil was in the army. Tax irregularities with his business had contrived to move him to Australia with his wife. Outstanding investigations had convinced him not to return. The blessing, on neutral soil, was a great excuse for the brothers to reunite.

Natasha once again stole the show in a beautifully tailored ivory silk pencil dress which ended just below the knee. The creator of the flattering garment was her best friend and former colleague, Sheila, who now stood behind her as chief bridesmaid, with Monica bringing up the rear.

With his beautiful bride, and with his misplaced brother by his side, any misgivings Neil may have had about the occasion were dispelled.

The surprise didn't end there. Behind the bridal procession, Neil's mum and dad, his sister, her husband Brin, their children, Natasha's mum, and John's wife, accompanied by their two children who Neil had never met, filed in. The blessing was to be a proper Curland family reunion.

## CHAPTER THIRTEEN

**Star man**

The blessing passed off without a hitch. In contrast to their wedding, the close family service in the tiny chapel was followed by a whole week of Curland family festivities, and then it was time to wave everyone off home.

Neil, Natasha and the kids had one last night of Warren's Texan hospitality, and then it was time for them too to depart.

The kids were sleeping on sumptuous Bateson extravagance; the two tots were unaccustomed to such opulence. They looked like a couple of crash victims spread out across the expansive beds.

Neil and Natasha strolled out onto the veranda, itself large enough to land a helicopter.

Gazing up at the clear nightscape with its romantic bounty of twinkling stars, Neil brushed his lips against Natasha's hair, sliding his arms around her slender waist. He nuzzled her ear and whispered, "Well, what do you think?"

"What do you mean?"

"We could have something along these lines, escape from the UK. This could be our back garden. Wouldn't that be something?" he softly elaborated.

"Oh Neil, it would, wouldn't it? I don't know, should we?"

"We should think about it. It would be a wonderful life. The kids would love it. If the TV show is a success out here we could move the whole kit and caboodle over here, televise the whole move. It could really work out."

Natasha pulled his hands, which had come to rest on her slightly swollen belly, down towards the valley of her sex. "You are such a hopeless romantic Neil. It turns me on so much." She turned to face him.

He leant forward to sweep her up into his arms, ready to whisk her off to bed.

"No Neil," she said. "Make love to me here, under the stars."

She lay down on the smooth boarded surface of the veranda. Neil lay down beside her, drew the straps of her thin summer dress down, and slipped her beautiful creamy breasts from within their confinement. Gently he played his rough fingers tenderly down the nape of her neck, along the silky smooth skin of her underarms, and on to the edge of her breasts. Her chest rose up as his fingers stroked the circumference of her nipples. He was fascinated by the reaction his caress elicited from his lover's body, how her breathing would labour as her heart sped up, how her nostrils flared to take in oxygen as the glands of her sex swelled in anticipation. This was the chemical reaction which would fuel his arousal, send the rush of hormones to the parts of his body the sexual act required. This time, Neil would take control, take Natasha to the stars, just like he'd once promised.

Natasha was arching her back, thrusting her pert, full breasts towards him as he kissed his way down her chest. Her large sensitive nipples were fully erect, demanding his attention. He pushed the dress down with his hands as his tongue explored the subtle curves of her belly and hips. The musky smell of her arousal renewed the vigour of his assault, and he lifted her bodily from the boards for his lips to taste the prize she proffered.

Resisting the temptation to straddle her for his own satisfaction, Neil put himself between her legs, forcing her to lay back and enjoy the pleasure he was offering.

With his mouth, he made love to her slowly; his smooth sensuous tongue circled the inner lips of her sex darting to and fro, just touching her clitoris with the occasional flick.

In a moment of inspiration he thought of the tiny padlock, fastened through the bar which was pierced through the hood of her clitoris, a Christmas present for him some years ago. Taking it between his lips, he passed the little metal lock between his teeth, sending a tiny static shock through the sensitive little bud and making her double up with the intense pleasure. He gently pulled the padlock behind his teeth, exposing her, leaving the precious little gland vulnerable to his assault. His tongue attacked without mercy.

Natasha lost count of the times she came, begging Neil to stop as her tormented body could take no more pleasure. "Neil please, make love to me," she begged. "Please Neil, I want you in me." Then, commanding, raw animal lust fuelling her impatience, "Neil, fuck me. Fuck me now!"

The sight of her sex, pulsating with savage desire, was too inviting for him. Despite his best intentions he couldn't resist her any longer, and plunged his throbbing manhood inside, between her pliant welcoming legs.

Her whole being was trembling with aftershocks as she suddenly started building towards a crescendo again. "No, no, nooo!" she sobbed as her body powered towards what seemed like the climax to end all climaxes. Neil's pace quickened as his excitement threatened to explode.

Their bodies crashed together in a cataclysmic explosion of shared emotion and bodily fluids as they screamed out their passion into the still of the night.

"Shit! Do you think anyone heard us?" Neil questioned, as his excited pulse began to slow its erratic rate. Natasha hugged him to her, acutely embarrassed. The two of them exploded into paroxysms of laughter.

## CHAPTER FOURTEEN

**Pregnant pause**

The short break in Texas numbered among the best times the family had spent together. Neil and Warren had bonded like brothers separated at birth. The appearance of the extended Curland family, in particular exiled brother John and family, had just been the cherry on the cake.

Nell, Warren's wife, was a rock. Living life in her husband's imposing shadow, she was not one to suffer fools gladly, preferring just to take her leave and allow Warren to play 'master of ceremonies' when she didn't bond with the company. She had blossomed around the Curland family, obviously loving the opportunity to fuss and pamper the Curland juniors and staying up till the wee small hours chatting with Natasha. Clearly, the younger woman's unpretentious honesty and surprising homeliness had struck a chord with Nell from the first time they met. She had taken the younger woman to her heart just as her husband had done.

As Warren and Nell waved the family off, Nell turned to her husband and said, "I think that gal's swallered a watermelon seed."

"You think?" Warren replied. "I'm not too surprised, the amount of practising they put in. They sure do know how to play happy families. I'm going to miss having them around, that's for sure."

## CHAPTER FIFTEEN

**Flashback**

The journey home was unremarkable.

Glad to be back on her own familiar turf after the best part of a month away, Natasha had dropped the children off at her mum's so that she could catch up on the chores of a dusty, neglected home. Her injured foot was not healing well. Since their return she had noticed that the wound had started to weep and that the area around the ball of her foot was very sensitive and surrounded with a red rash.

Sitting on the kitchen stool, she massaged the area around the puncture wound. Immediately, the wound began weeping a dark fluid.

Since the flight home, Natasha had also noticed she had a slight discharge; just a little spotting, probably nothing to be concerned about but it was enough to make her stall announcing her suspicions to Neil until she had confirmed that she was indeed pregnant, and that the baby was healthy.

Natasha's two previous experiences of pregnancy and childbirth had both been traumatic for their own reasons. Sharing the news of a pregnancy with a loving, supportive partner was not an experience she had been through before.

With the added worry of her foot, she decided a trip to the doctor was required. If he confirmed the pregnancy and that everything was OK, she would announce the happy news to Neil tonight.

She called the local surgery and arranged an appointment. Just as she replaced the receiver in its holder, the phone rang again, startling her.

"Hello?"

"Miss Caraccio?" a familiar voice questioned.

Surprised for a moment, unaccustomed to being addressed by her maiden name since her wedding, Natasha soon connected the voice with a name. "Eve? Is that you Eve?"

"Yes Madame, it's me."

"Eve, how are you? How's the studying going? Have you settled back in OK?" Natasha questioned, anxious to know how her former au-pair was doing.

"Madame, I need your help, I need to ask a favour of you." Her tone struck Natasha as grave, serious.

"Oh Eve, you can call me Natasha, you know I consider you a friend. Are you in trouble? How can I help?"

"Natasha. Can we possibly meet up? I need to speak to you face to face," the au-pair replied.

"Of course we can Eve, where are you, when were you thinking of coming over?"

"I'm here Natasha. Can we meet up somewhere now?"

"Right, well, I have a doctor's appointment in 10 minutes at the surgery in Exeter. Let me know where you want to meet up and I will get there as soon as I get finished at the doctors. Do you know Exeter at all Eve?" Natasha asked.

"Yes, I know it quite well," she replied.

"Where shall we meet?" Natasha asked.

There was a long pause before Eve answered. "I'll tell you a good place; head along Topsham Road, towards the swing bridge. You'll come to a road called Colleton Hill." Another long pause. "Go down to the water, then turn right, you can park along that road for free. I will meet you there and we can walk along the river to the Riverside café. We can talk on the way."

## CHAPTER SIXTEEN

**The gift of life**

The doctor examined Natasha's injured foot, turning it this way and that. He concluded, "You definitely have a slight swelling around the wound area. I think we will give it a good clean, dress it, and then give you a course of antibiotics, just in case there's any infection."

"What about the baby?" Natasha asked.

The doctor studied the results of the tests and the ultrasound scan. "Oh, don't worry, baby's just fine, everything appears healthy. The discharge is nothing to panic about, just a little spotting. Not surprising really with all the motorbiking, horse riding, flying hither and thither, different time zones and jet lag. It sounds to me as though you need to slow down a little. How are you coping with the morning sickness?"

"I haven't really had it. I've felt nauseous a few times. I don't really suffer morning sickness, I didn't with the other two either," she replied.

"Lucky you, my wife suffered terribly, or should I say, 'we' suffered terribly. As soon as she would start, it would start me off. I'm very squeamish for a doctor!"

Natasha laughed! "Will I be OK to take antibiotics, they won't harm the baby?"

"Amoxicillin won't do baby any harm. We don't want to chance mum getting a serious infection; that would put you both at risk." The doctor looked over the top of his reading glasses and his face took on a stern look. "Now, about that tetanus booster you were too busy to come in and have before you went off gallivanting!"

Natasha looked suitably cowed.

"Yes, we'll just administer that booster, in case there are any more rusty nails in the car park. I would consider it negligent of me to let you escape again without that!"

"But, the baby..." Natasha began to protest again.

"Pish and tish," the doctor interrupted. "The tetanus jab is completely safe for the both of you!"

Natasha hobbled out of the surgery with a throbbing shoulder to match her throbbing foot.

# CHAPTER SEVENTEEN

## Satanic rising

Natasha parked her BMW in a quiet cul-de-sac. She made a mental note to remember this place for further excursions into town. The road had once led to a bustling industrial dockland area. The commercial buildings had long been pulled down, and the area looked like it was earmarked for a housing development or even a municipal park. Right now, it was a vast expanse of deserted *'free'* parking. She could see Eve about two hundred yards away, sitting on a bench, overlooking the river. She was about midpoint between the car and the café. As she strode off towards her, Natasha immediately regretted agreeing to any walking; she had forgotten how painful her foot was.

The walk cost her more painful steps than she cared for, and she was looking forward to a sit down on the rather welcoming bench, before taking on the challenge of reaching the café.

"Eve, I'm so pleased to see you," Natasha remarked, embracing the young woman in a sincere hug.

Eve looked awkward, uncomfortable.

Natasha, suffering from the pain in her foot was too relieved at having reached the sanctuary of the bench to notice anything was amiss.

"Now what is this pressing matter you need my help with?"

Too late, she noticed the younger woman's distracted focus concentrated over her shoulder.

Sudden instinctive fear made her turn, just as Brian Dix leapt up from below the river bank. Natasha screamed and was already moving quickly, back towards her car.

She had a head start on him. Brian tripped as he tried to turn suddenly on the damp grass; his shoes, heavy and slippery from standing in the river water failed to make purchase and he stumbled down on to his knees. On a normal day, she might just have had the edge, might just have made it back to the safety of the car, to sanctuary, but today was no ordinary day; her injury slowed her usual fleet of foot, robbed vital seconds from her flight. She almost turned the key in the lock when she felt the weight of Brian Dix crash into her, knocking the wind out of her. She felt a sharp stab into the muscle of her thigh. Brian flung the used hypodermic down onto the tarmac and was dragging her back towards the bench. With every step she felt she was losing coordination, barely able to keep her legs moving to avoid falling down. As the figure of Eve loomed towards her, Natasha passed out.

Brian had planned well. The small boat was completely concealed below the river bank. Between the two of them, he and Eve dragged Natasha into the hull before exchanging a few words and parting company. Just down the coast, offshore of the River Teign, a bigger boat was waiting, one with both fuel capacity and seaworthiness to make the regular trips across the straits of the Irish Sea. Normally, this vessel would be making the trip under cover of darkness, carrying weapons and munitions from Ireland to the eager criminal gangs and traveller communities on the mainland. This time, it would be carrying its miserable human cargo on the return journey.

The small dinghy pulled alongside the larger vessel and manoeuvred to the rear where a low platform made it easier for divers to enter and exit the boat. Arriving unnoticed, Brian had to let out a low whistle before a head and shoulders appeared from the cabin of the boat. The crewman let a set of stainless diving steps down into the water.

Brian tied the dinghy fast to the steps, then set about lifting the prostrate figure of Natasha towards the outstretched arms of his accomplice on board the boat. As her jacket opened, Brian felt the stiff card in her inside pocket. Curious, he pulled the photograph from the pocket. It was a picture taken by the ultrasound machine; it clearly showed an image of a developing foetus. He noted the date on the scan was today's date; the name on the scan, Natasha Curland. Brian smiled; today just couldn't get any better!

## CHAPTER EIGHTEEN

**Becalmed**

Neil hadn't slept a wink since Natasha's disappearance. Reluctant to take a missing person's report seriously until 24 hours had passed, the police had just called round. Despite Neil's insistence that something untoward had occurred, the police still insisted on running through all their inane questions about whether she was suffering depression and whether they had argued recently. They left with a list of Natasha's close friends and acquaintances. Neil had been phoning everyone they knew, working his way through both of their address books.

He had marked out a hundred mile radius on the map and had been systematically phoning all the Accident and Emergency hospitals that fell in the catchment area.

Exhaustion had eventually given way to sleep. He was spark out with his head lying on the telephone table.

Startled, consciousness returning with a rush, the insistent ringing of the doorbell wrenched Neil back into the land of the living.

"Mr Curland?" the police officer asked.

"Yes," Neil answered.

"Mr Curland, may I come in?"

"Yes of course, please do," Neil said, showing the officer through to the kitchen.

"Mr Curland, we have discovered your wife's car down near the Quayside area of Exeter. Can you think of any reason she might be there sir?"

## Bittersweet Humiliation

Neil stood with his hand to his forehead. "No, I have no idea why she would be in that area; it's not somewhere we frequent. I can't think of any reason for her to be there. You haven't found her then?" Neil asked, fearing what the policeman's next words might be.

"No sir, we haven't found her." He paused, gauging Neil's reaction before continuing. "Sir, would you know if anyone might wish your wife harm, might perhaps wish to detain your wife?"

"You mean would someone want to kidnap her?"

"Yes sir, I suppose that is what I mean. Do you have any suspicions as to who might wish to abduct your wife?"

The policeman's line of questioning was becoming tedious to an exhausted Neil. "For God's sake man, will you just spit it out? Do you know something? Have you found something?"

"Yes Mr Curland. We do believe there may have been some sort of a struggle. Your wife's keys were found in the driver's door of her car. The key was bent over at a right angle but it would still have opened the lock. The door was still in the locked position." The policeman considered telling Neil about the syringe with traces of horse tranquilizer and the drag marks down to the water's edge, but decided against it, waiting instead to see what Neil's response would be.

"Oh dear God!" Neil exclaimed. He was thinking of Brian, but common sense told him that Brian was almost certainly dead. He said, "You must have seen my wife's file. There was an individual in her past that has kidnapped before, but the authorities believe him to be dead. My wife is a very wealthy woman, if she's been kidnapped it's most probably for financial reasons!"

"Mr Curland, with your permission, I think we should set up an incident room here in the house. If your wife has been kidnapped, there's a distinct possibility that the abductor will call with demands. The sooner we can set up an incident room, the better placed we will be to respond." The policeman waited for Neil to comment.

"Well don't just sit there, start organising it, we're already a day behind now," Neil shouted, frustration overpowering restraint.

The policeman bit his tongue and quickly exited the house to use the police radio in his car.

With the police officer out of the house, Neil placed a quick call to Warren.

## CHAPTER NINETEEN

**Wrath**

"Warren, it's Neil... Natasha has disappeared."

The receiver remained inert. Over the clicks and hisses of static, Neil could hear his own anxious pulse reverberating through the plastic.

"What the hell are you saying Neil? What do you mean, she's disappeared?"

"I don't know Warren, she got a call, went to a doctor's appointment, then she didn't return home. I haven't seen her since. She's been missing since yesterday."

"Oh hell Neil. Are the police involved? What do they have to say?" Warren was clearly distraught.

"The police think she may have been kidnapped. I don't know Warren, I think they know more than they're letting on. I think they may have me down as a suspect."

"I'm sure that's not the case at all Neil. What was she at the doctor's for?" he enquired.

"She was complaining about her foot not clearing up. The police are checking with the surgery to find out what they discussed."

"Oh, Jesus H Christ Neil, what can I do? What do you want me to do? Should I fly over? What say I organise a few top private dicks, fly 'em on over? Hell Neil, I feel as useless as a one legged man in an ass kicking contest!"

"I don't know what any of us can do right now Warren. We'll just have to wait, see what washes ashore."

Neil immediately regretted his words as the image of his beloved Natasha as a lifeless corpse flashed through his mind. Warren's reassuring tone snapped him from his morbid thoughts,

"Look Neil, I'll start ringing some doorbells, find out who I have to sleep with to get some top guns on the job there OK?"

"Thanks Warren. Anything you can do will be for the best. God I hope she's OK, I can't lose her again."

"Look after the kids Neil and keep me informed. I'll do what I can this end but let me know the second you have something."

"I will Warren. I will."

Neil pressed his finger against the hook and stared into space. His mind wandered back to the discussions he had had with Warren over religion. He wondered what he had done to incur the wrath of such a vengeful God.

Before the receiver had settled back onto its yoke, the policeman returned from his radio exchanges in the car. "Mr Curland?"

"Yes," Neil replied.

"It appears that your Mr Dix is still very much alive!"

# CHAPTER TWENTY

## Original sin

The ringer on the phone rang just once. Neil rushed over and picked up the receiver, praying silently for good news.

"So, Mr Curland, how does it feel being single again?" the unmistakable voice at the end of the line enquired, filled with vitriol and hate.

Realisation chilled Neil's heart. He recognised the voice immediately. "Brian."

"Full marks bastard," the disembodied voice replied.

"Why, Brian? Haven't you caused her enough suffering?"

"Oh this isn't about her; this is about you and me, Soldier Boy, about what you stole from me."

"What?" Neil stammered, struggling to take it all in.

"You took the bitch and you took my little girl." His voice had taken on a pronounced Irish accent. "Now I've got her back... And she's not alone, that was an unexpected bonus which makes us almost even, so it does... An eye for an eye."

"What are you on about?" Neil interjected.

"Don't tell me she hasn't told you Soldier Boy? You didn't know? Oh this is just fucking priceless!"

"What the hell are you on about you madman?"

"Oh, the lovely Natasha, she's up the pole again." He paused, allowing the enormity of his words to sink in. "Yer going to be a daddy again

Soldier Boy, so ye are. 'Cept it won't get that far, me boys will see to that, they'll fuck that little snapper out of her belly so they will." Brian's mocking tones spilled from the phone like acid. "Mommy's got to earn her keep."

"You fucking bastard, why can't you just leave her alone? I am going to track you down you evil son of a bitch. I'm going to rip your fucking heart out!" Neil was screaming into the phone, practically hysterical. "Let me tell you, mother fucker, if you harm a hair on her fucking head I will spend every penny I have, every waking moment until I've tracked you down."

Brian's evil laughter echoed down the receiver.

Neil's hysteria racked up a notch. "You fucking inhuman bastard." He paused, collected his thoughts. "I am going to kill you Brian, I'm going to really take my time."

"I look forward to it Soldier Boy. You just be sure to wait for my next call now, otherwise, I'll take great pleasure in posting bits of them to you in plain brown parcels." The laughter drifted off, replaced by the click of the receiver then the continuous tone of the dead line.

Neil knew instantly the seriousness of Natasha's plight. His first instinct was to contact Goose; bring the team back together and hunt Brian down.

He knew that Brian had planned the snatch too carefully, knew that their first assault had exposed the team's strengths and weaknesses. The last time they had the element of surprise; they'd been lucky. This time, Brian would know they were coming.

Thinking out of the box, Neil knew he would have to play to his strengths; money and Warren. With Warren's influence and CIA connections, Neil knew he would have the best chance of bringing Natasha home alive, bringing his unborn child home unharmed.

He picked up the phone and dialled the number he had memorised.

"Goose mate, it's Neil. I need your help."

"What's up Neil?" Goose replied, acknowledging the gravity of Neil's tone.

"Brian, he's still alive! He's kidnapped Natasha." Neil's voice wavered, but held firm.

"Oh shit, oh mate, I'm so sorry. Shit, I'd better make some calls."

"No Goose, just get yourself down here please. I have a plan but I need your support," Neil replied, his tone subdued.

"Oh bollocks." Goose suddenly remembered what he'd recently started in motion before receiving Neil's call. "I'd better make some quick calls before I leave. I need to cancel a shit storm that's about to kick off!"

"What do you mean?" Neil questioned, confused.

"Nothing, nothing at all mate." Goose was instantly embarrassed at the thought of the stupid, selfish act he'd been about to do. "Just a silly dry run; a moment of insanity. Nothing that matters now!" He shook his head as if the act would clear the madness from his thoughts. "Neil?"

"Yeah?" Neil replied.

"I'm on my way."

"Be careful Goose, the house will be a crime scene by the time you get here."

"Understood!" Goose put down the phone, then made a number of calls in quick succession.

Without too much explanation, he apologised to his friends for the letters, explaining them away as a drunken joke. It wouldn't pass close scrutiny with his intuitive friends, but it would do for now.

The next call Neil placed was to Warren Bateson.

"Warren. It's Neil."

"How is she? Have you found her? Please tell me you've found her Neil and she's OK?" Warren's voice was strained, emotional.

"Warren, it's Brian, he's kidnapped her."

"Oh Lord no." Warren exclaimed. "Jesus H Christ Neil, that man is meaner than a skillet full of rattlesnakes."

"I need your help Warren," Neil spoke quietly, gravely.

After a short, terse exchange, in which Neil brought the American up to speed on events, Warren replied, "Listen Neil, send me a telex with everything you've got on the man. All the contacts you used first time out, everything, try not to miss anything out. I've sounded out a contact on Capitol Hill, he'll see to it that everything lands on the desk of the best man to help!" Warren paused. "Neil is there anything you can do there? Can you go after him again?"

"God I want to Warren, I want to get over to Ireland right now, but my sensible head says he's baited the trap, he's waiting for me to walk straight into it. I'll have to wait, wait for his next move!" He took a sharp breath in. "Warren?"

"Yes Neil?"

"I'm going to offer him a trade."

Warren waited on the end of the line, waited for Neil to elaborate.

"I'm going to offer my freedom for hers!"

"Please give me a day to work the angles Neil, we may find a weakness in his armour. Don't do anything hasty, the scumbag would probably be happier to hurt you both."

## CHAPTER TWENTY ONE

**Time to wait**

By the time Goose arrived, Neil had brought the police up to speed on his conversation with Brian and they had locked down the house. They had their monitoring and tracing equipment in place as well as a specialist abduction agent who had briefed Neil on answering the phone and what questions to ask. Waiting for a further call from the rabid dog that was Brian Dix would prove to be the longest wait.

Goose hammered hard on the door. Sweat dripped from his body, his face etched with stress. His car sat on the drive, the metal ticking and groaning from the obvious caning it had received to get here in double quick time.

The two men embraced.

"Thanks for getting here so quickly." Neil glanced at the tension on his friend's face. "You look done in!"

"There's no quick way to get here that don't involve a big right foot. I got me collar felt on the fucking A30. Shat me packet sitting there with the boot loaded up with tools!" He gestured towards the car.

"Jesus Goose. What did you do?"

"Told 'em the friggin' truth, didn't I. Told 'em me mate's missus had been kidnapped, that the rozzers down here were dealing with it and I was on my way to help, any way I could."

"Well you must have sounded sincere, they let you through."

"Let me through. They only gave me a fucking blue light escort to the Wiltshire border. Imagine if they'd asked to see what was making the wheels touch the arches at the back? They'd have locked me up and chucked away the key for good!"

Neil shook Goose's hand again, genuinely relieved that he'd arrived safely. "What toys have you brought?"

"Didn't know what we'd need, so I brought everything!" There was no humour in Goose's voice despite the farcical nature of the statement.

"The bastard hasn't called back; I don't know what to do," Neil informed him.

"I say we get over there, get ourselves to a safe house and see what we can dig up. Same as last time; mobile, tooled up and ready to move."

"It's very different this time Goose. Brian was organised, the grab was carried out with military precision, and his intel was spot on. There's more to this than meets the eye. I'm not even sure he'll have gone to ground back in Ireland. Besides, I have to be here to receive his calls, otherwise he'll kill her. Goose, it gets worse; Natasha is carrying my child and the bastard knows it."

## CHAPTER TWENTY TWO

**Welcome to Hell!**

The drugs were starting to wear off. As feeling returned, Natasha's body ached all over from the confined space. Her hands, restrained behind her back with box tape, made her impotent to prevent her body impacting against rough edges inside the boot as the car pitched and rolled on the unmade tracks, causing her face and skin to burn from multiple scratches and bruises. Box tape covered her eyes, pressed into the sockets so she couldn't tell night from day.

Mercifully, the car came to a sliding stop. The cable clicked and the boot opened a crack; precious fresh air flooded into the space. Natasha's senses burst into life. She could smell trees; a forest. She could smell a wood fire.

Menacing voices circled around her as she was hoisted bodily from the boot of the car and dragged backwards by the armpits into a building. A stench of animals and rotting hay pervaded her nostrils. She was in some sort of farm building.

Rough hands grabbed at her sleeve, pulling it off, ripping the stitching from the shoulder. She felt a sharp scratch as a needle pierced her skin, then dizziness, followed by complete calm.

With no concept of time she awoke, again in darkness. Her body ached from her recent torments. Lying on a bed of hay, her wrists still tightly restrained, she became aware of insects and carrion crawling over her exposed limbs. In sheer fright, she kicked off with her feet, pushing her torso against the coarse surface of the walls. Slowly she worked her body upright and onto her feet. Still unsteady from the drug induced coma, she slipped on a patch of hay, wet with her own urine, and fell back to the floor.

Her condition, the smell and the revolting surroundings caused her to retch violently and she added to her own discomfort by vomiting down the front of her shirt.

A tiny pinprick of light pierced the weighty gloom of her prison. With its help she was able to feel her way around the filthy dungeon; the movement soon alerted her to the fact that she was wearing a stout chain, manacled to her ankle.

Her jail was a space of about twelve square feet. The walls were made of multiple hay bales stacked like bricks. Their sheer weight made the prison impenetrable. One wall seemed to be a solid lump of wood. She pressed against it with all her weight; it didn't budge, didn't flex. She pressed her back against the hay wall and tried to pull some of the wadding from the bales with her bare hands. It was impossible, the hay was so compressed it would cut her hands to ribbons. With the wall supporting her, she held the chain taut with her free leg, lifted her chained ankle and pulled back as hard as the pain would allow. Even if the prison were not impenetrable, the leg iron certainly was. The chain consisted of several coils. She could only guess at its length but it was made fast to a sturdy looking ground anchor set into the concrete floor.

Defeated, she leant back against the unyielding hay and sobbed, the salty tears burning as they found their way into the scratches criss-crossing her skin. Eventually, exhaustion robbed her of consciousness.

She awoke abruptly as the wooden wall was dragged open. Sunlight flooded into the stinking cell.

"Hey, wakey wakey, rise and shine." The mocking voice laughed, "Get yourself up, you smelly bitch."

Natasha was too frightened to move.

"C'mon, you dirty cow, get out of there! Look at yerself. You've pissed yourself like a wee baby. Get yerself out here, or I'll drag you out by yer fucking hair."

Blinking like a rabbit in headlights, Natasha staggered out of the stinking pit, out into the barn.

Producing a menacing switchblade knife, her captor, a large framed man in a black balaclava, cut the parcel tape restraining her wrists, before returning the knife to his boot. He grabbed one of the loops of the chain and dragged her forward, making the restraint short and fast to a corkscrew of metal, protruding from the concrete floor of the barn. This place was purpose made for the imprisonment of wretched humankind.

Natasha's eyes flicked around her surroundings, taking in as much information as she could; a cornered animal, desperately seeking means of escape.

Too late she noticed the fire hose her captor pointed at her. She took the full force of the freezing water in her face and chest. Her eyes burned from the force of the jet, her lungs were robbed of oxygen, and she fought a desperate battle to avoid drowning. She lay on the concrete floor on her back, her head aching from the force with which she had hit the floor. She knew it was the end as the water forced up her nostrils and into her airways. She tried to twist away in a last ditch attempt to find air for her tortured lungs but the chain was at full extent and held her firm. Just as she was losing consciousness her experienced torturer, now in fits of mocking laughter, cut the pressure.

As she coughed the water from her lungs, and gulped in life giving breaths, her tormentor spoke. "There we go now, that's better. Now you smell a little less like the pig ye' are."

"Why are you doing this to me?" Natasha sobbed between breaths.

"Because yer a dirty little soldier whore, that's why," he said, with a voice filled with hatred. "I'd kill you now if it were up to me, but the boss wants you alive, so he does." He added, "Alive I will do, doesn't mean you have to be comfortable though does it? Oh I'll keep you from dying sure enough, but when I'm finished, you'll wish I hadn't."

"For pity's sake," Natasha implored, "I'm pregnant. Please, for the child's sake, don't hurt the baby!"

The savage face leaned in close to her and said, "That's a British baby yer carrying; a soldier's baby, no less. 'Tis the fucking anti-Christ itself."

Natasha looked into his eyes and found not a shred of compassion.

"Don't you worry yerself girl. You won't be bringing another fucking little Brit soldier boy into the world, we'll see to that. Now get those filthy clothes off!"

"What… no," Natasha stammered.

"Get the fucking clothes off now otherwise so help me I'll stick this fucking hose down your throat. Undress… NOW!"

Terrified out of her wits, Natasha did as she was told. She undressed quickly, avoiding being coy or nervous, keeping her shoulders hunched so as to disguise the curve of her breasts, taking care to make the act matter of fact, not at all titillating. Nevertheless, she could feel her captor's eyes on every part of her body. She unfastened the short wraparound skirt and dropped it to the floor; her underwear remained captured by the chain.

Her captor strolled over to her and crouched down between her legs. She was straining the chain, trying to put distance between them, trying to pull away as far as possible, but keeping her legs pressed together.

He reached down into his boot and withdrew the switchblade. In one deft movement the ultra-sharp weapon sliced the knickers through, and he slung them across the barn.

Standing up abruptly, he pressed the evil blade between Natasha's legs.

"Don't look at me like that you bitch," he snarled. "If I wanted your dirty little hole I would fucking take it." He took a step forward, applying more pressure to the knife. "I wouldn't touch you with a bargepole, you little British whore, especially when there's a fucking British soldier's snapper in there already!"

Keeping the blade forced against her skin, he sliced it across the flesh before closing it and putting it back into his boot.

## Bittersweet Humiliation

Natasha dropped to her knees. Shock registered on her face and she involuntarily reached between her legs, waiting for the inevitable rush of warm pain.

The pain didn't come. He'd used the back of the blade.

"That was a warning whore," he laughed. "Next time, you won't be so lucky!"

He walked back across the yard before returning with the hose again.

"This time, I want to hose you off. I can't stand the smell of you, so it can't be too pleasant for you either. Make it difficult and I will give you full power again. Make it easy and it will be over quicker."

Natasha did not fight him, she let him hose her body all over with the freezing stream of water until he was satisfied she was clean. He then trained the hose onto the floor of the makeshift cell, sluicing the soiled hay out through the open wall.

He tossed Natasha a pitchfork and instructed her to gather some fresh hay for the jail floor.

The thought passed through her mind to attack him with the pitchfork. A quick mental calculation told her that he was keeping well clear of her limited range.

She picked up her skirt; along with a fork full of hay, and threw it into the cage without her captor noticing.

# CHAPTER TWENTY THREE

**Tracks**

The police returned with a van full of bodies and equipment. Neil brought the detective in charge up to speed on the phone conversation with Brian Dix. The detective was no fool, and had taken the intuitive step of pulling the file on Brian Dix, reading it on the drive over. Within an hour the police were set up and had pretty well taken over the house. Their equipment was about as sophisticated as you would expect from a rural force. The technician connecting up the phone tapping equipment was explaining to Neil that he would have to keep the kidnapper talking for a few minutes for them to accurately trace the call. Goose was not impressed.

"Neil," he whispered, "the gear they have here is hopeless; I've connected up a trap."

Neil looked puzzled.

"It's a portable AMA system; we can get the billing information from the relay center the second the call connects. The billing centers have been switched digitally since the mid-eighties. Trust plod to be still working in analogue."

Neil trusted Goose. Intelligence gathering was his trade and he really knew his craft.

The phone rang. The assembled bodies instantly erupted into a flurry of activity, starting tapes and throwing switches.

Goose sat calmly, not moving a muscle. His box of tricks, courtesy of Star Net, had engaged automatically, silently and was already on the case, attempting to follow the call back to its digitally created invoice and the recipient of said invoice.

"Hello?" Neil questioned.

"Hello Neil," the menacing voice answered.

"Brian!"

"Listen here Soldier Boy; you and the bitch are good and rich so ye are. I'd say some of that lolly is rightfully owed to me. I figure you should be able to raise a bob or two between the two of yous, so I do!"

"I'm not cash rich, my money's in the business and property, but I'll pay whatever it takes if you'll let her go unharmed. I beg you Brian, if there is still a scrap of humanity left in you," Neil pleaded. "She's still the mother of your child. You must have cared about her once, for pity's sake, let her come home to her family."

"Ah well, that little speech has touched me heart. I was going to just choke the bitch right now, but knowing how strongly you feel, I think I might just take me time then Soldier Boy. I don't mind looking after the lovely Natasha for a bit, give me a chance to get reacquainted with the missus after all. Tell me Neil, does she still like you to stick yer finger in her arse when she comes?"

"You fucking bastard, I'm going to fucking tear your head off and shit down your throat!" Neil's composure was gone out of the window.

"That's better, I prefer the arrogant British soldier," Brian laughed. "The sensitive husband doesn't suit you. Here's a peachy deal for you Mr Curland, you come and rescue the fair Natasha, then you'll get your chance Soldier Boy, to be sure, you'll get your chance, but we'll be seeing who shits down whose throat so we will. Don't take too long though Mr Neil, 'cause I've got a number of nasty acquaintances lined up here, and what do you know, they all fancy having a crack at your pretty little wife!" Brian's maniacal laughter crackled in the receiver. "Ta ta Mr Neil, we'll speak again soon. I've got an itch that needs scratching and your wife's tight, naked ass should tickle it just right. Bye now."

With that, the phone went dead.

Brian Dix smiled to himself. At present, he had no intention of demanding a ransom for Natasha. Living on the lam, under the protection of the IRA, it was impossible for him to keep the presence of big money a secret. Even if he managed to pull it off, and disappear, they would know. It would complicate his life, make him a target for every two bit crook and scumbag on the street. No, this Natasha assignment was both business and immense pleasure. Worst case scenario, if his plans were discovered before reaching fruition, he could wave the offer of a ransom demand under his bosses' noses. With any luck, his nemesis Neil Curland would fruitlessly chase after his beloved and Brian would taste the ecstasy of a double revenge.

# CHAPTER TWENTY FOUR

**Threats**

Natasha lay in the darkness of the hay cage. She had no concept of time, only the terror of awaiting the unknown; whatever was to come. Sleep came in fits and starts only when exhaustion defeated the awareness of horrific anticipation. The sodden skirt she had risked all to retrieve seemed like the only remnant of her former life, her dignity. Despite the total desperation of her situation, wearing the little skirt represented the only protection she had against the hopeless vulnerability of her nudity.

The heavy wooden door was dragged to one side. A pinprick of sunlight pierced down through the aged opaque plastic sections in the asbestos roof.

Natasha's pupils fought to adapt to the sudden demand the light brought on her retinas.

The man stood in the doorway of hay. The sunlight framed his silhouette, making him appear angelic; her salvation perhaps. Her desperate mind told her Neil had found her. When the figure finally spoke, it was with the unmistakable Irish drawl of Brian Dix. All hopes were instantaneously dashed.

"Oh my pretty, look at you here, all humble. Where's your airs and graces now Mrs Curland?"

Natasha cowered in the corner of the cell, her arms wrapped tightly around her chest, shielding her naked breasts from his scrutiny.

Brian turned to her captor. "Did you scrub her down good?"

"Aye, she's clean," Balaclava replied.

"Good. Michael, get your arse over here."

Brian's right hand man, his lackey, rushed over to do his boss's bidding.

"Get the gaffer tape from the car Michael."

"Brian, please don't hurt me," Natasha pleaded. "Brian, I'm having a baby. I beg you Brian, please, don't hurt my baby."

"*Shut up! Shut up!*" he screamed, lapsing into the maniacal tones which Natasha knew so well, and feared above all else.

There would be no reasoning with him.

The lackey returned with the tape.

"Right then, tape up her wrists."

"Brian, please Brian… No," she begged.

"Tape up the fucking whore's mouth too. If she can't keep it shut, tape the fucking thing up." His mood became ever more menacing. He picked up a hay bale and threw it into the cage. With another one stacked on top, he grabbed Natasha by the hair and dragged her towards them. Pushing her over the bales, he shouted to Michael, "Hold the bitch's head down."

Natasha could only whimper into the tape gag as Brian Dix lifted the back of her short skirt. She heard him spit on his hand, felt his rough wet fingers as they parted the lips of her sex, then she felt the hot pain of shame as he delivered her first helping of humiliation; it was a recipe she would come to know well.

Satisfied, he pulled out of her. "Your turn Michael!"

The lackey smiled and carried out his boss's orders with gusto.

Natasha was breathing heavily. The initial severe pain of the violation had passed. The barbaric savageness of the assault was beginning to sink in. In her mind she was focussing on an earlier time in an attempt to protect her fragile psyche. She was remembering the business meetings she had conducted, all the men who relied on her, relied on *her* to make shrewd business decisions, to provide food for their families' tables. Right now that counted for nothing; these monsters were using her like an animal, and like a cornered and outnumbered animal she had no will but to succumb. She lay still and prayed they would finish soon.

When Michael had filled his boots, Brian gestured to Balaclava, who was massaging a bulge in his trousers, clearly brought on by the degradation of Natasha. "C'mon you, yous gets to take a turn too."

Balaclava shook his head. "No way Dixie, I'm not going there, there's a fucking snapper in there so there is, a fucking British snapper at that, I'm not doing that, so I'm not."

"*Get over here and fuck this bitch!*" Brian screamed, the malevolence in his eyes enough to strike fear into the heart of the bravest of men.

"I'm not doing it Brian; I'd burn in hell if I put my cock in next to that wee snapper so I would," Balaclava protested.

"Well if that's all that's bothering you, you can shove it up her arse then, but you will fuck her, so ye will, otherwise I'll fuck you!" He turned to his lackey and snapped, "Michael, hold her down."

Accepting the compromise, Balaclava unleashed his enormous engorged member from the confines of his combats and proceeded to savagely jam it into Natasha from behind. When the weapon found its goal, he shoved with all his considerable might. Natasha screamed out in pain; a pitiful muted sound, baffled as it was by the strong tape. Twisting her wrists until they bled, she desperately tried to wrench a hand free from her captor. The previous indecorous submission extinguished by the agony of this unnatural act, she fought back bitterly, desperately trying to extract herself from this vicious onslaught. Ultimately it was a futile struggle against superior forces. In exhausted resignation she screwed her eyes shut to erase the grinning faces of her tormentors.

Brian Dix laughed out loud as Balaclava pumped furiously without end in sight.

"See this Michael? This man has a hidden talent so he does. We shall have to remember to use him for all our anal de-flowerings from now on." Squeezing Natasha's contorted face to open her eyes, he laughed, "Get used to it honey, this is what you do from now on!"

# CHAPTER TWENTY FIVE

## Miscalculation

"Bugger," the technician swore as his equipment failed to connect all the dots before the line was cut.

Goose put a hand onto Neil's shoulder in commiseration. His eyes directed Neil's gaze towards his hand which was discretely gesturing a 'thumbs up'. He snuck out to his car, but when he returned the disappointment was evident on his face. "Damn Neil, I'm so sorry. There was one simple thing I didn't consider; he used a pay phone. I didn't even think of that." He punched the air in frustration. "Damn! How could I be so stupid?"

The insistent ring of the phone galvanised everyone into action. With a nod from the detective, Neil picked up the receiver. "Hello?"

"Neil, it's Warren. Any news?"

Neil held the receiver to his chest and reported to the police and technicians, "It's a friend, a private call."

The technicians stood down.

Neil brought Warren up to speed on the recent conversation with Brian.

"Listen Neil, I've got some real clout in the Senate and the corridors of power over here, players who have direct access to the CIA and, in a roundabout way, the IRA. We would have a lot better odds if we had you over here, overseeing the information as it came in."

"I'll see what I can do Warren. It's pandemonium here at the moment; I think I will struggle to slip away. I'll have a word with the guy in charge of the investigation, see what he thinks."

Neil took the detective to one side.

"I need to travel to the States. Is that going to be a problem?" he asked.

"Is there a pressing need for you to travel Mr Curland?" the detective replied.

"If I'm going to be required to raise a large ransom, I will need to speak to the money men in America, see if an advance would be possible."

"Can't you make arrangements over the phone Neil?"

"I think it's going to be an uphill struggle to convince them to advance me any large sum of money face to face. Over the phone, I'd have no chance," Neil assured the detective.

Doing his best to be tactful, the detective replied, "Neil, I don't think it would be appropriate for you to leave the country right now. We haven't got anything resembling a formal ransom demand, just a vague threat. We need you here as this thing develops. Your input and background information will be invaluable to the investigation; I couldn't possibly let you leave the country now."

Neil was in the mood for an argument. "I really think I would be of more use over there, trying to raise funds so we can move quickly when the opportunity arises."

"Neil, I'm sorry, but kidnapping is a very serious crime." He hesitated. "I don't know how to put this. Your wife is a very wealthy woman, she's been abducted and at the moment, everyone is a potential suspect!"

"Well, thank you for your candour, so now it's official, I'm a suspect?"

Nicholas P Boyland

"I'm sorry Neil, I can't let you leave the country, not now."

# CHAPTER TWENTY SIX

**Red tape**

"I've been on to my man in the US Consulate Neil, I'm afraid your Home Office have dug their heels in. Kidnapping and abduction of UK citizens is a serious deal. My man over there is a really big player but he can't get them to budge an inch. They are insisting that this is their investigation and they aren't willing to share any information regarding it."

"Warren, I'm completely hamstrung by the authorities here in the UK. I can't travel at all; they've taken my passport away. I can maybe get Goose to fly over; he knows a fair bit about Brian and his cohorts."

"That would be something Neil. It's a damn shame Natasha's not an American, if she was, we could get jurisdiction over the case and I'm sure we'd have no problem getting them to play ball."

"That's it Warren! You've got it!" Neil exclaimed.

"Well if I have, I'll be jiggered if I know what it is," Warren replied.

"Natasha is Italian!" Neil announced. "She was born in Milan. She's an Italian citizen."

"Well that news is sweeter than stolen honey Neil. The Italians are as crooked as a dog's hind leg. Leave it with me, I'll make some calls, wake us up some eye-talians. I reckon you can go pack your toothbrush Neil." Warren was ecstatic; his obvious enthusiasm left Neil optimistic as he hung up the phone.

The British authorities were not easily coerced into handing over the investigation. The detective in charge of the investigation spoke to Neil; his manner was quite openly hostile. "I hope you know what you're doing Mr Curland. We have good relationships with the Royal Ulster Constabulary, and with the Garda. You claim that Mr Dix has in all likelihood abducted your wife and is holding her somewhere on the island. By having your 'VIP' friends pressure us off this investigation you could well be signing her death warrant." As a final threat, he added, "I have to caution you Mr Curland, if the investigation goes sour and life ends up lost, you are still a British citizen and subject to the full weight of the law."

"Don't you think I am trying to do the best I can for my wife?" Neil replied, with more than a little vitriol. "My 'VIP friend' has resources at his disposal that you could only dream about!" Neil's voice, rising to a shout, conveyed the anger he felt. "If you had been willing to be a little more flexible, we could have combined forces. Unfortunately, with you people it's them and us. You are the law, everyone else is a client. My 'VIP friend', or rather his friends, are used to working with multiple agencies. I believe my wife has a better chance with them on the case, and if that means we pull strings to take the investigation away from you, then so be it."

"Be careful who you make an enemy of Mr Curland," the detective threatened angrily.

"Oh please," Neil retorted, "do you think I give a flying fuck about upsetting you? What are you going to do, follow me home and smash my tail lights with your truncheon? Arrest me for having had one too many wine gums at the office Christmas party? I couldn't give a crap if you lock me up; throw away the key if it gets my wife back unharmed. If you can bring her back to her children in one piece then you do it, for fuck's sake. Do your worst!"

The detective coloured from the tips of his ears to the nape of his neck.

"I'm sorry Neil, I realise that was uncalled for." In a more conciliatory tone he added, "I sincerely hope that your 'connections' are successful in returning your wife to you safe and sound. I'm sorry we are not able to participate any further in the investigation. Perhaps you would inform the agency that takes over the investigation that I would like to be kept abreast of developments, and will be happy to cooperate in any way I can." He handed Neil his card with his personal phone number on it before adding, "There is considerable bad feeling among the hierarchy in the force over this issue Neil, some of the 'blue bloods' put their heads on the line to keep this investigation and they aren't used to being overruled. I warn you, they may throw obstacles in your way out of spite." He offered Neil his hand. "I wish you well Neil. I hope you get your wife back OK."

Neil soon learned what the detective's warning related to. In a small minded scheme to stall the proceedings, the British authorities attempted to prevent Monica from travelling to Austin with Neil and her brother. Only timely intervention by Natasha's mum, as Monica's legal guardian, prevented them from putting a spanner in the works, and Neil, the two children and Goose would soon be on their way to Warren's ranch.

## Bittersweet Humiliation

Neil would need to make a call to Janice, his PA at the office of Copper Road Choppers. Janice was fully up to speed with the unfolding events.

"Copper Road Choppers, Mr Curland's PA speaking." Janice sounded tired and emotional, as if she was a heartbeat away from floods of tears

"Janice, it's Neil."

"Neil, have there been any developments?" she asked, concerned.

"It looks like we're cleared to go. Nothing more positive, I'm afraid."

"Neil, I'm so sorry. I'm praying for you both."

"Thank you Janice, it can't hurt."

"Is there anything that I can do Neil?"

"Just keep an eye on the lads and keep things ticking over here please Janice. Oh and could you please look out for mail, here and back at the house. We've got a special re-direct at the post office, but just in case anything slips through, anything, no matter how trivial or unimportant it looks, please courier it straight over to Warren's place in Marble Falls. Don't open anything, just put it straight into another box and have it sent over special delivery. Anything work related I'll send straight back to you once it's been examined. OK?"

Janice simply grunted an affirmative; she could barely speak for crying. She would do whatever was necessary. "Good luck Neil. Please bring her home."

"I will try to Janice, I swear, I will try." Neil put the phone down.

## CHAPTER TWENTY SEVEN

**Comatose**

The cocktail of drugs her captors had administered to her rendered Natasha into a semi-comatose state.

It was a formula the Provo pharmacists had honed to perfection, giving the debilitated victim the power of movement without the will to fight or flee. A chemical frontal lobotomy.

In the dead of night, a bruised and bloody Natasha was transferred from the barn to a dark stinking room in a secret brothel. It was a place where only the clandestine customers were free to come and go, and the wretched inmates wouldn't leave while they still drew breath.

Michael handed custody of Natasha over to a middle aged woman, Corinne. She was old beyond her years, but through a triumph of sharp wit over decaying looks she had managed to elevate herself to the position of madam.

"Jesus, Joseph and Mary, just look at you. I'll bet you were once a grand lady so ye were. You must have made yerself a proper nuisance for them to want to bring you down like this."

She took a long look at Natasha, saw the far staring eyes and the vacant expression.

"Oh Be'Jesus Michael, not another ghost. How am I to make a working girl of them when you've got 'em so strung out they don't know which end's for sitting on," she complained.

"This un's a special case. Dixie wants her worked hard," he replied.

"What's the bloody point? Nobody's going to get any pleasure out o' her the state she's in, and *she* won't know if it's number four or forty."

"Like I said, she's a special case." He shuffled his feet, clearly uncomfortable with the woman's tongue lashing. "Dixie says she's to be given to the… difficult clients, the ones that like things a little… rough or unusual."

"Gonna have to be the Russians then, they don't give a toss as long as the pussy's warm. Dixie can be an inhuman bastard sometimes. What's the poor mare done then?" Corinne questioned.

"Rumour has it she's the mother of his kid. Don't go telling anyone I told you that."

"Jesus, Mary and Joseph, the poor mare." The compassion soon faded from her face. "Aye, well c'mon girl." She shooed the errand boy out. "Away wi yous! I better get started on this one, I can see I'll have me work cut out, so I will." She strutted away, dragging the incognisant Natasha by the arms behind her.

# CHAPTER TWENTY EIGHT

**Moving mountains**

With his passport returned to him and both children cleared to travel, Neil and Goose wasted no time in catching the first available flight to Texas, which happened to be a military flight from Fairford USAF base, courtesy of Warren Bateson. It was slower than the studio Lear but it was already in the UK, only an hour away and ready to fly.

Within fourteen hours, Neil had the children tucked up in bed, the blackout blinds and the air-conditioning fooling them into a jet-lag free, natural sleep. Neil, however, was keen to get started with briefing Warren's assembled team of crack agency men, which included a criminologist and an expert in counter terrorism who had done a tour of duty in Ireland with the British intelligence services. The Italian authorities had instructed an envoy from their US Embassy to observe. He had yet to make an appearance.

Neil brought them up to speed with what he knew of Brian Dix from his association with Natasha through to his gun running activities and his Provisional IRA involvement.

"With regards to our foray into Ireland, I'm not in possession of all the details of the intelligence corps contacts and the like. My associate Goose, Mr Geoff Duckworth, is the one to speak to with regards to names and ranks. I'm afraid I was somewhat distracted during our trip." Neil handed the chair to Goose, who, with his encyclopedic memory, was able to recall an astonishing amount of important and trivial detail about the mission to rescue Monica.

At the end of the briefing the atmosphere had changed from experts interrogating witnesses to a gathering of equal minds sharing information. Neil was convinced he had done the right thing by moving the investigation across the Atlantic.

"I want to get over to Ireland. I need to be there on the ground, doing something, anything, knocking on doors if need be," Neil declared to the CIA agent in charge.

"It might come to that Neil. If your Mr Dix wants you badly enough, you may be our 'ace in the hole' to lure him out," the agent replied.

"No, I want to get over there now and start searching. I can't just sit back in a comfy chair while that lunatic posts parts of my wife back to me in plain paper packages!"

"Neil," Goose interrupted, "we feel your pain mate, but time's moved on. I don't have the connections in the intelligence corps anymore. We go over there with what we've got and the best we can do is retrace our steps from our last sortie." Goose took a long breath and pressed on, pacing the floor as he spoke. "We know that farm lot was a fit up job to disappear Brian, so we know he's not going to be anywhere near there. What does that leave us, huh? A whole lot of fuck all, in a country that's every bit as big as England, somewhere we don't have a hell of a lot of friends."

"So we leave Natasha hanging do we?" He punched the air. "Jesus Christ Goose, I wouldn't want my worst enemy in the company of that bastard. We know what he's capable of!"

"Look Neil, he must have cared about her once, he's not going to hurt her; she's the mother of his kid for God's sake! He's trying to get you out in the open, luring you out, getting you so wound up that you go crashing around over there in a big white suit with crosshairs drawn on it." Goose was angry; his normally calm demeanour was tense with the emotion of the last few days. "We calm down Neil, we calm down and we plan, we strategise, we work with these CIA boys. They have ties with and intel on the Provo's that we can only dream about." He put a hand on Neil's shoulder. "I promise you mate, when the time is right for you to go stand in the open with a red flag in your hands I'll be there, on the high ground with an AW50, watching your back."

## CHAPTER TWENTY NINE

### Working girl

After the first day in the stinking dark room, Natasha had soiled herself. Corinne telephoned Dixie's errand boy.

"She's bloody gone and shit herself. It's no good Michael, you can't go stoking her up like that so she can't even take herself for a coodle. I'm not her bloody mummy. She's gone and shit up a good little skirt and a pair of stockings, let alone the bedclothes!"

The errand boy laughed. "I'm sure the Russians will pay good money for that."

"It's not funny Michael. I'm not washing these girls' bottoms. You'll have to stop dosing her up so much. Let the poor wee cow use a few of her remaining brain cells!"

"I'll see what the boss says Corinne." The line went dead.

Eventually, they managed to fine tune the medication to the point where Natasha was just about able to control her bodily functions and at the same time satisfy the carnal needs of a steady flow of scum who were willing to pay to use the body of an attractive 'zombie'.

Such was the level of her stupefaction that the passing of days and the coming and goings of her clients meant little to Natasha. All that registered was the increase of pain before fixes and the euphoria afterwards.

On about the tenth day, she awoke from a trance-like state. Desperately needing her next fix, she was aware of her surroundings, aware of hunger and thirst, aware of pain. The heavy set man was lying between her legs, energetically pumping in and out. He was her tenth 'client' of the day.

Her arms hurt where he had them pinned down. The muscles in her thighs ached. A fire burned between her legs.

The Soviet was the size of a house. He fell onto her with all the finesse and subtlety of a rutting rhino. Three quarters of a bottle of neat vodka had done nothing to dampen his ardour and his massive weapon of assault was functioning just as nature had intended.

Despite the absence of energy in her muscles, Natasha was feeling every wave of pain inflicted on her. The cocktail of drugs made her tongue and throat feel swollen; blocked, robbing her of coherent speech, leaving guttural moans her only means of communication.

The Russian was thoroughly enjoying himself. With the tools nature had endowed him even working girls felt tight. This one was no exception!

He was obsessed with her breasts, squeezing them so hard with his massive hands until his fingers met, leaving them purple with bruising. The nipples grotesquely protruded, puffed out to the size and shape of ripe strawberries. He sought out the fruit and hungrily sucked it into his mouth, chewing and drawing on it as if it were a fine cigar.

Well into her third month of pregnancy, Natasha's tortured body was going about the business of creating a sustainable life. The glands in her breasts were readying themselves for the task of producing nutrients for a healthy newborn. Colostrum was being produced, waiting for the suckling of a hungry baby to demand fulfilment. Thinking that moment had arrived, the little miracle factory released the nectar into the lips of the suckling offspring.

The Russian disembarked as though he had been shot through the jaw. First incomprehension, then pure unadulterated fury registered on his hate distorted face.

He shouted in his mother tongue, "You damn dirty bitch."

Throwing Natasha off the bed as if she were a sack of potatoes, he rained blows down upon her with his massive fists.

By the time his rage was spent, Natasha lay in a bloodied heap on the floor.

## CHAPTER THIRTY

**Broken**

Her next 'client' came into the room just after the big man left. He took one look at the broken body on the floor and ran from the room shouting, "It wasn't me. I didn't do it! I'm fucked if I'm copping for that!"

Corinne ran in, alarmed by all the commotion. She saw Natasha lying there and in genuine shock, exclaimed, "Oh Jesus, Mary and Joseph. Oh what the fuck have you gone and done girl? Oh no, just look at yourself... *JANINE*!" she shouted. "*JANINE!* Get yourself in here girl."

"Corinne, what is it? Oh Jesus God. Is she alive?" the girl asked.

"I don't know, I don't know, I think so... barely. Get that fecking eejit Michael on the phone, get him over here now!" Corinne was crying through her cursing. "Oh God Natasha. C'mon girl, don't you dare die on me now!"

Natasha came to, clutched at her belly and staggered to the filthy porcelain lavatory in the corner of the room. She retched, vomiting blood and teeth into the bowl. She clutched her belly again as a spasm of pain gripped her into a doubled up squat over the filthy bowl.

A further massive spasm gripped her abdomen and the little miracle, created some three short months before to a promise of a lifetime of love and devotion, was extinguished.

# CHAPTER THIRTY ONE

## No respite

"Oh Jesus! Oh Jesus God forgive us! Oh God, we'll burn in the pit of Hell for this, so we will! Oh the poor little mite!" She stared at the human remains in the bowl. "Oh God, Jesus, Mary please forgive me my sins! Oh God, oh the poor wee mite!" She sobbed out her guilt and shame.

Natasha slumped to the floor. Mercifully, her tortured body had shut down and she had slipped into unconsciousness.

Janine ran back into the room, looked into the toilet bowl, screamed and pressed the flush repeatedly until the obstruction was gone.

"No Janine. No!" Corinne shouted as she realised what the younger woman had done. "Oh Janine what have we done? The poor wee mite. Oh, we'll burn in Hell so we will, for sure."

Suddenly thinking clearly Corinne said, "Janine, get a pillow between her legs to stop the bleeding. I'm going to get my car. We need to get her to a hospital before she dies."

"Michael's on his way, we should wait for him," Janine protested.

"She'll die if we don't get her to hospital now Janine. I'm not going to meet my maker with the blood of both of them on my hands. Please, help me get her downstairs then watch her while I get the car."

Between them they managed to drag the inert Natasha onto the back seats. Corinne jumped into the driver's seat as Brian Dix slammed the passenger door shut.

## Bittersweet Humiliation

"Drive Corinne," he snapped, his voice devoid of emotion.

"Oh Jesus, Mary and Joseph Mr Dix, the wee baby. Oh Lord, we'll surely burn in Hell so we will. I'm taking the poor lass to hospital; she's just about all done in."

Brian wound the passenger window down a crack. "Well done Janine, you did good, I won't forget." He turned his gaze back to Corinne, a pistol pressed into her ribs. "Now Corinne, I said drive. I'll tell you where to go!" Brian was furious. Everything hung in the balance. He had plans for Natasha with her spectacular looks. She was to have been a big earner in the brothel; he was confident she would have pulled in the punters, given him some ammunition to use with his superiors if he was called upon to justify the risks he had taken to bring her in. If she died now, without having seen a positive return, it would go down as another one of his fuck ups. Worse still, they would discover that he was working on an outside commission and his last ditch negotiating card, the ransom demand, would die with her.

# CHAPTER THIRTY TWO

## Beelzebub

The barn where she had been held captive was about half an hour away. Natasha did not regain consciousness during the drive.

"Get out," Brian commanded Corinne. "Grab her arms and drag her out of the car, into the barn."

Corinne did as she was told. A wiry woman, used to living on her wits, she could summon a great deal of strength when she needed to.

"Mr Dix… Brian, we need to take the poor girl to hospital; she's just lost her wee baby, she'll die if they don't treat her."

"Maybe she will, maybe she won't," he said, callously. He put the muzzle of the gun to Corinne's temple and said, "You, on the other hand, definitely will!"

He pulled the trigger. In the confines of the barn the retort was deafening. Mercifully, Corinne didn't hear it. She stood still for a while, somewhat puzzled by the fountain of crimson flowing over the hay bales in front of her, and then her world went dark forever.

"Clear up this mess Michael," he commanded. "Then call the vet over here to make sure this mare survives. I want her fit to go back to work as soon as possible."

## CHAPTER THIRTY THREE

### They shoot horses, don't they?

Natasha was laid out on a cold stone table in the corner. Made from the same concrete screed as the floor of the barn it was easy to sluice down with the pressure hose, which was handy as in the normal day to day running of the farm it would be used for occasionally operating on livestock, or for illegal slaughter.

The 'vet' was up to his shirt sleeves inside the belly of his first human patient in some time. Things were not going well.

By the time he had crudely sewn up the untidy incision in Natasha's belly, the small pile of discarded human tissue he had amassed in the filthy porcelain sink did not hint of an encouraging prognosis.

He held his bloodied instruments under the stream of water from the single cold tap and mopped the sweat from his brow.

With the tools packed away inside his bag, he turned his attention to washing the human remains down the waste pipe.

"Is it sorted?" Brian asked.

"Aye, after a fashion," the vet answered.

"What's that supposed to mean?" Brian enquired.

"Hell, I'm used to fixing up bullet wounds. I've no clue about the human female anatomy. 'Tis fecking complicated. She was a bloody mess in there too, all screwed up. She lost a lot of blood. I've had to cut off all the busted bits and sew everything up. Not my tidiest work!"

## Bittersweet Humiliation

Brian raised an eyebrow. "So will she live?"

"Oh aye... Possibly, most probably... I've stuck a drip in her arm and given her some strong antibiotics. She won't need to worry about birth control anymore though, that's a dead cert!"

Brian laughed. "In her profession, that's a bonus." Greatly relieved, he slapped the vet on the back and walked out of the barn, singing, "Everyone's a winner baby that's the truth!"

He got back into the car belonging to the recently demised Corinne, and was about to start the engine.

"Before you bugger off," the vet shouted after him, "I'm not staying here with her. You will need to keep her warm now, and see to it she stays clean. Keep the wounds clean at least; that is, if you want her to survive the night. I've used soluble stitches inside and out so you won't need me again, but you will need to give her some basic nursing care to make sure she survives." He could see the exasperated look on Brian Dix's face. "Feck it, your call, I've done my best." The vet gathered his things, got into his car and drove away.

Brian cursed and turned to his lackey, who was getting into the car beside him. "Jeezus, isn't this whole incident becoming fecking tedious? Michael, get her into the farmhouse, feed her up with some broth or something, look after her; no more shit until she comes around fully, and then make sure to keep her stoked. We don't want her getting it into her head to try a runner now do we?"

## CHAPTER THIRTY FOUR

**Filthy whore**

It was weeks before Natasha returned to the brothel. Physically she had recovered but psychologically she was lost, her spirit broken. Michael recognised this and cut her drug regime to just addictive narcotics. He knew that with her will broken she would be easy enough to handle; willing to do anything for the next fix.

At Brian's insistence, she was handling twice as many 'clients' as the other girls. The abuse was taking its toll on her body. She had aged considerably in the time she'd been in captivity. Her hair was falling out in handfuls. The bones of her hips, shoulders and ribs protruded through the skin.

Her clients complained about the unsightly scarring on her stomach, the missing teeth and the way she writhed in agony as they sought their pleasure.

Janine, who was now the madam, reported back to Brian. "I'm having to let her go fast and cheap," she laughed. "The men like the girls to suck them a little before they get down to business but she can't do it no more 'cause it makes her choke. See, she can't breathe through the nose no more, not since that big Russian gave her his wee bit o' lovin'."

Brian smiled at the news. "I don't care how you do it Janine, just you make sure she earns us big coin."

"We could give her to the arse men, I suppose, seein' as how her front bottom's been sorta ruined. She looks better from the back than from the front now anyways," she sniggered.

A thought crossed his mind. "Film it, Janine, film the final humiliation of that little whore, and be sure to get it all on VCR. I might just have a customer for that," he laughed, sardonically. "If her little Soldier Boy doesn't come for her soon, there'll be nothing left to rescue."

## CHAPTER THIRTY FIVE

**Salvation**

There was one man among Natasha's 'clients' who had taken a shine to her, a tall, handsome Irish traveller called Aiden. He called her his 'Broken Angel' and would spend time using her tenderly, paying Janine for extra time to spare her from her usual string of visitors.

Natasha subconsciously responded to his compassion. She would wash herself thoroughly in the filthy sink before his visits. She would hug him tightly as he availed himself of her body and sob uncontrollably when it was time for him to leave.

One night, Natasha woke to find Aiden standing at the end of her cot. It wasn't unusual for Janine to send gentlemen callers to her bed at all hours and she resignedly threw back the covers and opened her legs in submissive readiness.

"No Natasha, I've come to get you out of here, take you away. You're coming with me now!"

"No, they'll kill us both," she said. It was the first time she had spoken in months. Her voice was little more than a harsh rasp.

"Aye, that's a fact. They'll have to find us first though, so they will. There's no love lost between my people and them. My folk will not give me up so easily."

Even in her brainwashed, defeated state, Natasha could recognise that Aiden offered a better option than the fate facing her here.

"Janine is downstairs pissed as a newt. Neither the Devil nor Lord God himself could rouse her. I slipped a little 'Micky Finn' into her nightly grog, so I did! The rest of the girls will hold their tongues. They know not to speak out, not to get involved."

As they passed through Janine's quarters, Natasha rushed towards the tall metal cabinet against the wall, recognising it as the safe which held the madam's stock of drugs. While a stupefied Natasha hammered her fists against the unyielding steel in a futile attempt to extract the hidden nectar, Aiden, with the power of rational thought, rifled through the madam's purse, took a key from it and unlocked the cupboard which was screwed to the wall. He grabbed the few vials, syringes and packets of white powder that lay inside along with any other paraphernalia he could lay his hands on and shoved them into a carrier bag.

As they reached the car, Aiden instructed Natasha to lie on the back seats with her arms behind her back. She did as she was told without question. He secured her wrists, feet and mouth with box tape before covering her with a blanket.

"It's for your own good," he said. "Can't have you shouting out. The Paramilitaries here shoot first and ask questions later."

They drove for some considerable time on tarmac before the road ran out. They continued driving for some miles further up a green lane track before Aiden got out of the car to open a field gate.

Across the field they arrived at their destination. Natasha could hear the chatter of children playing. It stirred some distant memory of a former life, which was quickly forgotten amongst the drug addled mess which represented reality in the here and now.

Aiden lifted her out of the car and cut the ties from her legs and wrists.

She could smell wood smoke. It was the first time she had been outside in months.

Her craving was overpowering; she reached into the carrier bag which had been left on the back seat with her.

"Not so fast," Aiden chastised. "I'll be taking charge of those just to make sure you behave yourself. You take care of my needs," he gestured towards the bag of drugs, "and I'll take care of yours! You'll be needing a lot more than this to keep you going, so you'd better make sure you keep me sweet."

Natasha had swapped one form of slavery for another.

The news reached Brian that Natasha had gone. He was livid. Initially, he believed that Neil had outwitted him again. It became apparent, after an extensive 'interview' with Janine and the girls, that Natasha's abduction was from within the Irish traveller community. A quick review of the video tapes confirmed his suspicions. He couldn't risk an inter-family war with the Irish travellers right now so close to home.

Brian decided to let it go. He had long since bored of Natasha; her earning potential had dropped since her 'troubles'. It appeared that he had got away with his little dalliance with the outside commission. Besides, it didn't look as though Neil was going to rise to the bait. No, he surmised, it wouldn't have been long before he would have sent her off to be with Corinne and the baby, better to let her be someone else's problem. He knew the Gypsy community, knew that her 'saviour' would be unlikely to release her. No, it was more likely that she was to be kept as a slave, pimped out or sold on. At best, she would be kept around until her abductor tired of her, then he would probably off her himself.

'Good riddance,' he thought.

He fondly caressed the video tapes; there was a shipment of guns sailing for the mainland shortly and he could get one of his henchmen to drop a box off at the post office while he was there. Time for one last pop at Mr Neil Curland, see if the tapes wouldn't be the final insult that would push him over the top. This way, even if Natasha did shuffle off her mortal coil at the hands of another, at least Neil Curland would be in no doubt about the part Brian Dix had played.

How Brian wished he could be there when Neil opened the box!

# CHAPTER THIRTY SIX

**Out of the frying pan**

At the Gypsy camp life settled into a routine. Natasha cooked, cleaned and skivvied for the other families in the camp. In return, she lived without fear of further beatings.

Aiden, true to his word, kept her cravings stoked. Despite the constant pain she was in, his reward was the gratitude she showed him in bed. On the face of it, their relationship resembled that of a couple, but in reality the drugs and her addiction kept Natasha's mind from focusing on anything past or future. The isolated, remote location of the camp would have made escape difficult, even for one in possession of all their faculties and a clean bill of health. Natasha's mental state meant that her only actions were those necessary to facilitate the next fix.

Her problems started up afresh when Aiden took an interest in a young traveller girl from another family.

The girl's father convened a meeting between the two families.

Both families crammed around the table in Aiden's mother's caravan.

The father, a hirsute brute of a man spoke first and got straight to the point. "You cannot court my daughter while you keep fer yerself a fecking concubine."

"She's no bloody whore; she looks after meself and Ma. She works around the camp too," Aiden defended.

"I'm having none of it. You've grabbed my little girl, now if yer keeping yer promise to her, you've got to please her mum and take her down the aisle. Get shot of the Buffer whore."

The father was not up for hearing any excuses, it was an ultimatum. Breaking his promise to the girl would mean a family rift, which could lead to bloodshed.

Aiden formulated a plan whereby he could have his cake and eat it too. Natasha had healed up quite well. A good supply of healthy food and fresh air had brought back the vitality to her looks. By installing Natasha into another brothel, one he was a patron of, he could still visit her when the mood took him and earn a little commission off her too.

To make her a little more compliant he upped the level of heroin coursing round her veins and set his plan into motion. Unwittingly, he had started a chain of events which would ultimately lead to Natasha's salvation.

"Rules is simple here," the madam said, "the more tricks you do, the more gear you get. All my girls is addicts so they all work the same score. Take too much, you'll end up sleeping through the timetable and make no tricks. So you get no shit! Got that?"

Natasha nodded.

"Yeh, you get it all right, you been around the block girl, I can tell. You got a big habit going, huh? Just don't you go stealing gear from any other girl! You want it, you gotta earn it. OK? I'll keep you stoked, and I'll make sure you don't overdose on the stuff. You just keep your tricks happy and we'll all get along just fine."

After a few weeks at the new brothel, Aiden's visits ceased. His future in-laws were keeping him under constant surveillance now. The upside was the brothel madam, an Irish American, had given him a generous price for Natasha.

Thanks to her habit, Natasha was soon turning twice as many tricks as the previous 'best girl', much to the delight of the madam. The sex caused her considerable pain but the shit fixed the pain. The sex bought the gear so an unholy alliance was formed.

Eating, drinking and even hygiene soon became secondary considerations for her and within a few months she had relapsed into a barely coherent automaton, living only for the next fix.

One of the brothel's infrequent clients had noticed Natasha during a visit and had returned the next night, specifically requesting a visit with her.

"Why would you be wanting to spend yer time with her?" the brothel madam questioned, naturally suspicious that one of Natasha's 'quickies' would want her again so soon. "I've got some much classier girls you can bide yer time with for sure."

"No thank you missus all the same." He lowered his voice. "I like to hurt the girls a little, so I do. This one, she's very submissive, timid like. Not all brassy and vulgar like t'others, do you know what I'm saying?"

"Aye. Oh well, whatever floats yer boat. Just don't be messing her up in the face. I'll be giving her away if you mess up the face any worse, to be sure."

## Bittersweet Humiliation

He saw himself up to the dingy room Natasha occupied. Natasha was busy with a client when he arrived on the landing, so he waited for the man to leave before letting himself inside.

Natasha lay on a filthy cot; she didn't stir or turn and acknowledge him as he walked into the room, just lay with her legs apart, staring into space.

The man sat down on the bed beside her, wiped a vein in her arm clean with a square of alcohol soaked tissue and withdrawing a syringe from his pocket, injected the contents into her arm.

"Sorry, love," he said. "I'm afraid I've got to be cruel to be kind."

## CHAPTER THIRTY SEVEN

### Rescue

"Missus, missus!" the man shouted. "Missus, get up here!"

The madam ran into the room. By now, Natasha was half off the bed, convulsing, foaming at the mouth.

"What the hell have you done?" the madam screamed.

"What should I do?" the punter asked.

"Get her the hell out of here. Whatever you've done, it's not landing on my doorstep, get her away from here!"

"I'll dump her outside the hospital; they'll know what to do."

The madam quickly agreed, not wanting Natasha to die in her house.

"I'll tell 'em I found her wandering around. She'll likely die anyways so no worries it'll come back around."

He had no such intentions. By an incredible stroke of good fortune and diligence, the man was a CIA informant; one of the men in the pay of Warren's contacts, charged with the task of tracking Natasha's whereabouts down.

As soon as he had her inside his car, he pulled another syringe from the glove-box. Jamming the needle straight between her breast bone and her ribs, he injected the adrenaline straight into her heart. Instantly, the convulsions stopped. He held a photograph to her face, compared the likeness, then exclaimed, "Jesus girl, I nearly didn't recognise you! What a bloody mess, what the hell have they done to you?"

He drove at speed to the local hospital.

## CHAPTER THIRTY EIGHT

**Deliverance**

Neil and Goose were sat in Warren's den discussing progress when the all-important call came in.

"Warren Bateson." Warren's facial expression turned from mild indignation at the interruption to a fixed, deadly serious expression. "How is she?" Now everyone in the room was leaning forward in anticipation.

Neil's heart was in his mouth. From the look on Warren's face he knew that this would be the most important call of his life. He studied every line and every muscle on Warren's face, straining to pick up the slightest indication of whether the bulletin imparted good news or the end of life as he knew it.

"I see." He was keeping the conversation short, clipped. Talk on the phone was not secure. "You know the arrangements? Please get her to the airport as soon as she's stable enough to make the trip. I will have everything in place both ends by the time she gets there." There was a long pause while Warren listened to the man at the other end of the call share what information he had. Warren cupped the mouthpiece and mouthed to Neil, "She's alive. Natasha's alive!"

Neil was beside himself. Tears rolled down his cheeks and he began to sob uncontrollably. Goose held his hand firmly, his arm around Neil's shoulder conveying reassurance.

Warren spoke words of praise and gratitude into the receiver and replaced it on the hook.

"She's alive Neil, she's alive," he reiterated, scarcely able to believe his own words. "She's been through hell, she's in a terrible state, but she's alive." Warren's own tears were flowing freely now, down the big man's all American, action hero face. "We're bringing her home."

"The baby Warren, what about the baby? Did they say if the baby's OK?"

Warren stared at Neil. He instinctively put his arms around Neil and held him tightly as he gently whispered, "There's no baby Neil, I'm so, so sorry."

Neil wept now, wept for the suffering of the child he would never know, wept for Natasha, for the hell she must have been through, wept for himself, for the loss of that little piece of their love they had created and Brian's hate had destroyed. The tears washed away the sadness. In its wake, bitterness flowed into the void; bitterness and an overwhelming desire to make the perpetrator of all this sorrow suffer the same fate.

"Have they caught Brian?" Goose asked.

"No, I'm afraid not," Warren sighed. "Job for another day. Let's just bring our girl home!" Natasha's extraction had been extensively planned for, even when it was nothing but a faint hope. Now all that remained was for Warren to make the calls and put the carefully laid plans into motion.

Within hours of the hospital stabilising her vital signs, she was in a helicopter bound for Cork airport where a jet was standing on the tarmac, fuelled up and waiting with a medical team on board. Destination: Seton Medical Centre, Austin, Texas.

Natasha was flying back to the arms of her loved ones.

## CHAPTER THIRTY NINE

**Withdrawal**

The reunion was a shock to the system for Neil.

Acting on the doctor's advice he had kept the children away. He was glad of his decision.

Natasha was in a shocking state. Her only moments of lucidity were spent screaming and cursing at anyone within earshot because of the convulsions she was suffering as a result of withdrawal.

"What's the matter with her?" Neil questioned the medics.

"We need to get her started on a methadone programme quickly. She's too weak to face withdrawal yet. We need to get fluids inside her before she goes into shock again."

Neil was ushered out of the private room as the shutters were pulled around her bed.

Natasha's screams and oaths could be heard down the corridor. The doctor began to speak as they walked towards his office. "We've carried out extensive tests on your wife Neil. The good news is that she's tested negative to HIV and Hepatitis C. There are no signs of Leukoencephalopathy or Endocarditis. She has no signs of any immediate life threatening diseases. She has sustained a great deal of superficial and skeletal damage. She has several broken ribs which have not fused correctly. Her lower jaw has been broken and left to knit out of line, her nose has been broken and set crookedly preventing her from being able to breathe through her nose at all. She has a number of teeth damaged. Two have been smashed at the root and allowed to decay in situ. She has a large abscess growing under one of the rotting teeth which has eaten almost through her lower jaw bone."

Neil's face had turned as white as a sheet.

"The upside is that there is no external scarring at all on Natasha's face. Her facial nerves are intact and there is no soft tissue damage."

"What does that mean in layman's terms Doc?" Neil questioned.

"Well, we don't want to subject Natasha to any more procedures than strictly necessary at this time. However, I think it would ease her suffering considerably were we to bring the orthodontist and orthopaedic specialists into theatre, try to put everything right at once, so to speak. We need the jaw bone set correctly and the problems with her nasal cavity sorting as a matter of urgency. Failure to do so will exacerbate the healing. I will bow to the advice of these specialists, but if at all possible, it would be prudent to have dental implants introduced as soon as possible too, so that your wife's appearance is less of a shock to her when we lift the sedation. That's the good news over though I'm afraid." The doctor paused.

"Go on," Neil interrupted impatiently. "What's the bad news?"

"You might want to sit down; there is quite a lot of bad news."

Neil sat at the desk, his head in his hands.

The doctor followed suit and opened a thick folder.

"She has a strong narcotic addiction which we need to address immediately. She has some cirrhosis of the liver which has led to scar tissue forming, impairing the organ's function. Some regeneration will take place but for the most part it will be scar tissue which does not replace the healthy cells, this we can help with medication. She has contracted Hepatitis B which is treatable along with the liver damage, but unfortunately, not curable." The doctor looked at Neil, not sure if he could take any more bad news.

Neil sat with a stunned look on his face, close to tears.

"May I continue?" the doctor asked.

"Please," Neil answered.

"She has at some time in the recent past suffered a violent miscarriage or perhaps a forced termination. As a result of this procedure, it would appear that she has received some kind of medical intervention which, at best, can only be described as butchery. Neil, I am sorry to tell you that your wife's reproductive organs have been badly damaged."

Tears were flowing freely down Neil's face. "Can you help her?"

"Once we have her stable and calm we can go inside her and have a look at the extent of the damage to her liver. It may be possible to remove the scar tissue and leave the healthy liver to regenerate. I am afraid her damaged organs represent an immediate risk of infection. She may need to undergo a hysterectomy. Our options are limited, without taking substantial risks with her life."

"Is there no chance that she could ever conceive?" Neil asked, desperate.

"Neil, I have been practising medicine for over thirty years, ten years as a senior surgical consultant, and I have performed, assisted with, or sat in on gynaecological procedures too numerous to mention. I have never seen a case like this one. I am truly amazed that your wife has survived up until now without professional intervention. Her organs are so inflamed and damaged they could rupture at any time. Of course, you can sit down and talk it through with my colleague Dr Crispen who is our chief gynaecological surgeon. As things stand, Natasha is not capable of conceiving, nor is she capable of sustaining or nurturing a human embryo in any way. Without emergency intervention, it'd surprise me if she would be able to sustain her own life for much longer. The way she's been damaged, she's like a ticking time bomb. I'm just surprised she hasn't gone off already. I am sorry Neil, I truly am. I'm afraid the worst is yet to come," the doctor warned.

Neil sat, ashen faced. "Could there possibly be anything worse?"

"She has a hairline skull fracture Neil, at the front of her head, in the frontal lobe region. It's highly likely that this portion of her brain has sustained bruising or rapid acceleration damage similar to what we see in car accident victims."

Neil could hardly take in the serious extent of her injuries. He knew from his own experience that even minor brain damage may have potentially robbed him of the chance of having his Natasha back, ever!

"Can you do anything for her?" Neil asked, his voice a hushed whisper.

"The fracture is linear Neil and exhibits no fragments. We do not need to intervene, just keep her calm and see she avoids strenuous activity for a few months, give it time to heal. After that, we can X-ray to make sure it's healed smoothly. I know from your own experiences you're knowledgeable when it comes to brain trauma so I won't elaborate, just to say that we are hopeful that no significant damage was sustained to the frontal lobe. We won't know that for certain until she is fit enough to undergo psychological evaluation." The doctor stood up and walked over to Neil. Standing beside his chair he put a hand on Neil's shoulder. "Neil, I won't try to kid you my friend, she's unlikely to come out of this without deep psychological damage. This is the worst case of mental and physical abuse I've witnessed in my entire career."

"It would have been better for her had she just died. I can't bear the suffering she still has to endure," Neil admitted.

"Don't you ever think that Neil. She has fought so hard to stay alive, what right do any of us have to decide she would be better off dead?"

Neil immediately felt pangs of guilt for even thinking those thoughts.

"I firmly believe her strong will to survive indicates that there *is* something left worth saving Neil. You should embrace that belief and nurture it, for Natasha's sake." The doctor showed Neil to the door.

# CHAPTER FORTY

## Damaged goods

Warren rushed over to comfort Neil as he came stumbling out of the consulting room.

"Neil, what is it, what did he say?" the big Texan questioned.

Neil pushed him away, unable to convey his feelings in words, frightened that his friend's kind compassion would reduce him to blubbering like a baby. Like a baby, something which he and Natasha would never know again.

It was a full hour before Neil could speak. Warren just waited patiently giving him time and space to come to terms with whatever the doctor had said.

"Warren?" Neil sobbed.

"Yes Neil?" the big man answered.

"He's broken her Warren. Smashed her body, broken her spirit, and if that wasn't enough, he's taken away her power to create life. Everything that woman was about was being a mother. He's stolen that from her Warren, torn it out of her."

"Neil. God almighty, I'm so sorry, the poor girl."

"He has to pay Warren. We have to bring him to account for what he's done!"

"Yes we do Neil. Yes we do, but not now. Right now, you gotta be there for that poor young woman lying in that hospital bed. You gotta be there for those two little ankle snappers the Mrs is minding right now. You just stick around and make their mommy well again."

"She has a fractured skull Warren. Her brain is almost certainly damaged. We may not be able to make her well again!"

Warren paused for a second before replying, "You make her well again Neil, and then, and then," Warren paused again, taking a deep breath. "I swear this Neil… then we go after that somebitch and we teach him to tango!"

# CHAPTER FORTY ONE

## Barren soil

Dr Crispen called Neil through to a spacious, light and friendly office. All around the room were pictures of his family, memories of happy times at camp, grandchildren with smiling cherub faces, carefree laughter, family barbecues; all things which seemed remote, impossible dreams for Neil and Natasha.

"Neil, sit down, please."

Neil sat down on the sumptuous leather sofa, trying his best to stay rigid and upright, as if the impending news would be too much to take in a relaxed position.

Dr Crispen wore some kind of half-moon shaped reading glasses, generally more suited to old ladies. He looked up at Neil over the top of the frames. "We have reason for hope Neil. The surgery went better than expected. My team has managed to tidy up the damage which was inflicted on Natasha. I can safely say that as long as we have cleared up all existing infection and she suffers no further complications, her life is no longer in danger." The doctor glanced down through the lenses perched on his nose to study the notes he had made in a ledger. "The otolaryngology team has done a fine job on Natasha's nasal cavity. No external scarring; the organ should return to full functionality and we're optimistic that once the swelling goes down it should be as aesthetically pleasing as it ever was." He consulted his notes further. "The jaw bone has been re-set in alignment." He glanced up at Neil, pulling the glasses down his nose to better focus. "We have an exemplary orthodontist resident at the hospital Neil, he has designed a honeycomb denture splint which he has screwed to the void in Natasha's jaw bone. As the bone regenerates, we're optimistic that the dental implants will be encapsulated within the bone growth."

He read on from the ledger. "The results from the gynaecological team were not quite so encouraging. I'm afraid it's looking like the chances of Natasha being able to conceive or carrying an embryo to term are slim. There are techniques we can try, certain procedures, combined with a course of hormones to make the environment more conducive to conception. There is also In Vitro Fertilisation which may prove to be a suitable course of treatment in Natasha's case. In the meantime, she needs time for the wounds to heal, to see if her body will return to its natural cycle. That, I'm afraid my friend, is one for old Father Time and the lap of the Gods." He quietly closed the ledger and glanced back up at Neil. "Dr Hartford has asked me to direct you to him when we're through here, he has more pressing things to cover with you. Is there anything I can help you with now, anything you need me to clarify?"

"Is there a chance that she may be able to fall pregnant again?" Neil said, his voice barely a whisper.

"Anything's possible Neil. The human body is truly remarkable and life has a way of succeeding. I've done my best with the skills the good Lord has blessed me with. She will recover if it is God's will." With that, the doctor put a hand on Neil's shoulder and led him out towards the waiting receptionist. "Gail, could you see Mr Curland to Dr Hartford's office please, he's expecting him."

## CHAPTER FORTY TWO

**Dependant**

Neil kept pace with the receptionist down the short corridor; his legs felt like they belonged to some remote being, his mind felt near to meltdown.

"She needs to go into rehab Neil, you can't fix her at home," the doctor said. "No matter how strong you think you can be, watching a loved one suffer withdrawal will break you."

"I want her home, surrounded by the people who love her. We can help her through it," Neil argued.

"No Neil. You are not hard enough to take what's coming. She's been kept on a regime of methadone since she came to us to help stabilise her. What she needs now is complete withdrawal. Believe me Neil, I specialise in drug rehabilitation and I am telling you, the behaviour the drugs bring out as they leave the system is terrifying for loved ones, you would see a creature you wouldn't recognise. You must let us take her through these first stages. When she is finished here, that's when she'll need you most, when you can do her the most good. Please Neil, it's for the best. Hand her over to us. We will look after her and have the best chance of bringing the Natasha you remember home to you."

"That's not very likely after the ordeal she's been through," Neil replied, subdued.

"One step at a time Neil," the doctor reassured. "She's already come a long way with her recovery, let's get the poor girl clear of this heinous addiction now, then we can try to reverse the psychological damage."

"How long will it take?" Neil asked.

"To kick the physical dependency? About eight to ten days." He looked thoughtful. "The mental dependency is another matter. It could take months, years even."

Neil looked puzzled.

"Look Neil, Natasha is addicted to heroin, now it may well be that because of the circumstances involved and because her own lifestyle is so far removed from what you would consider typical, she may fight the cravings herself and stay clean."

"You're talking as though my wife were nothing more than a lousy druggie; this is my Natasha you're talking about, she's a businesswoman, a devoted mother, not some dirty lousy skank!"

"Neil, don't you think all 'druggies' start out as someone's daughter, someone's mom?" the doctor argued. "Heroin levels the playing field Neil; it cares not if you come from privilege or poverty."

Neil sat with his head in his hands.

"Natasha will always be a recovering addict Neil, I'm afraid that's something you have to face. There is never a one hundred percent success rate with rehabilitation; it's always the will of the patient."

"Natasha has no will anymore," Neil replied soberly.

"Well that's something you will have to work on Neil. You'll have to bring back her will to live otherwise you will surely lose her again one way or the other."

"How long do you think the whole process will take?" Neil asked.

"Her treatment here will take about six weeks, and then we can transfer her to the clinic. They have a resident psychiatrist, Dr Regina Ward, whose work with my patients I greatly admire. Dr Ward will be able to help Natasha through the cravings and the other mental trauma. She has spent time in the Third World, working with victims of people trafficking and slavery, and she is well versed in the kind of suffering your wife has endured."

Neil got up to leave. "OK Doc. I will sign Natasha over to your care, just as soon as she's well enough to leave the hospital."

As he walked back to his car, Neil tried to keep his mind focused on the immediate; helping Natasha piece her shattered mind and body back together.

Deep down in the pit of his stomach, he ached with a rage to keep the promise he had made to Brian Dix. For now, that would have to wait.

Back at the ranch and deep in thought, Neil picked up a large box; it had re-direct labels on it and was addressed to him. Since Natasha had been found, Neil had taken to opening his correspondence himself instead of taking it straight to the CIA lab as he'd been doing prior to her return. The outer box was marked with Janice's familiar handwriting. The box inside was marked up as containing video tapes and it bore a Southampton postmark; that was nothing suspicious, Neil frequently received video promos from all over the country.

Warren had a video cassette player rigged up to a giant CRT projector in the den; Neil popped the tape into the front and fired the machine up.

Goose was walking past the den on his way back from the loo. He hadn't heard Neil return to the ranch. The flickering lights and strange sounds reminded him of the cheap porn theatres he'd once visited in Amsterdam, during his days in the RAF. Curiosity got the better of him; the door was ajar so he carefully pushed it open and quietly walked in.

Immediately, he saw his best friend Neil lying on the floor crying his heart out. Goose looked up at the images on the screen. "Oh Jesus Christ almighty!" he exclaimed and stabbed his finger at the off button.

# CHAPTER FORTY THREE

**Consequences**

"Mr Dix, do you know who this is?"

"Feck, yea, I know who ye'are!"

"Mr Dix, you were engaged by my client to carry out a simple task and dispose of some merchandise. It seems you have failed, and the merchandise has turned up safe and sound in America!" The disembodied voice carried a polite but powerful threat.

Brian Dix felt his throat constrict. "Yea, sorry, seems she gave us the slip. Give me a bit of time and I'll see to it that you get yer money back."

"Mr Dix, did I ever imply to you that our arrangement was 'sale or return'?"

"Look, there's not a lot…"

The metallic voice from the earpiece interrupted, "Mr Dix, you have a job to do, nothing has changed except the venue. My client will cover your extra expenses in dealing with the changed location."

"Is it even worth it? The bitch is nothing but a shell, she's so fucked up I doubt she'll ever be able to remember her name," Brian replied, clearly tired of the game.

"Mr Dix, I feel you may underestimate the reach of my client. I can see that we will have to remind you of the sanctity of a contract. We will be in touch." With that the connection cut and the earpiece returned to its inert state.

"Aye, you do that you fucking wog fucker, who the fuck do you think you're talking to?" he screamed into the moulding before smashing it into a thousand pieces on the tiled worktop.

Brian hadn't left the flat for days. He couldn't travel to America. Without this commission being sanctioned from above he had no access to forged travel documents, let alone the contacts and safehouses he would need while he was there. Now he had lost all his cards. If the client pushed it, and his controllers found out, he'd be for the high jump. If he didn't do the job, he'd have the damn 'flip-flops' to deal with. He had been on a horrendous downer since the phone call. It wasn't easy for him, suffering like he had since childhood. 'Manic depression' they had labelled it, after one of his frequent stay-overs at one or another sanatorium. He had never bothered much with the fancy labels the men in white coats had given him. As far as he was concerned, his dad was always out thieving or womanising and his mother, always on the move, palmed him off on the doctors because she couldn't cope, or just couldn't be bothered with him.

His head was thumping from the effects of dehydration. He didn't look after himself very well when he got like this. Staggering to the fridge, he opened the door and grabbed the first bottle of milk he came to. He should have smelt the pungent odour of the sour liquid, but nothing really worked right when the fog descended!

The putrid milk assailed his taste buds at precisely the moment the door was kicked in. With the bile in his stomach reacting against the onslaught of vile sensation in his mouth, he was taken completely by surprise. Caught mid gag reflex, and before he could even comprehend the events unfolding, he was knocked to the ground. A hand was holding a wet rag against his face and there was an acrid smell of gas. Brian passed out.

## CHAPTER FORTY FOUR

**Amputee**

"Left handed or right handed?" the masked man shouted.

"What the fuck?" a surprised, groggy Brian retorted.

"Left hand or right hand you cunt, *now*, or I choose for you!"

"What the hell are you on about, you fucking bastard?" Tense and frightened now, Brian's voice had all but lost the Irish accent.

"Thumb or index finger?"

"What the fuck?" Brian's eyes were darting about, frantically searching for a way out, anything which might offer a glimmer of hope!

He was sitting backwards on one of his high backed kitchen chairs; his torso was wrapped with gaffer tape, firmly attaching him to the upright back. His feet had been forced through the legs of the chair and were taped up behind the front legs and the cross-bars. Movement was not an option.

"Thumb or pussy finger?" the mask shouted, his tone emphasising that it was his last chance.

"Finger… finger," Brian whimpered. "Wait, for feck's sake, wait." Cold realisation rose up through his mind like an icy fog. "I'm right handed. I'm right handed!"

Mask's obscured features tightened into a grotesque smile as he pulled the fingers of Brian's left hand apart. His damp, clammy fingers were separated by the edge of the worktop. Mask slowly applied pressure to the meat cleaver which sandwiched the index finger of his left hand between it and the worktop. At first, there was no sound except the low moan which escaped Brian's lips. Then, as he applied a little more pressure, there was an audible crack as finger bone and sinew joined flesh in parting company with the rest of his hand.

Brian stared at his mutilated digit in disbelief.

"There now, that wasn't so bad was it? Now then, I have a message for you. You're a fucking embarrassment. You've been caught moonlighting. If that wasn't bad enough, you fucked up and missed the mark. Now the army's involved. You're back working for us now, and you had better fulfil the contract! The client is insisting that *you* complete the job otherwise I would off you right now! You have a month to recuperate, and then someone will be in touch to give you instructions to finish the hit." Mask lent in close to Brian's tear-streaked face. "I'll be taking this little feller with me," he said, waving the finger before Brian's bewildered eyes. "Now just you be sure and get the job done, or I'll be back for some more bits."

Brian Dix, the hard man, the villain, the cold hearted killer, fainted!

## CHAPTER FORTY FIVE

**Recall**

A searing light burnt into Natasha's retinas. She tried to shield her eyes from the glare but her wrists were pinned down. Her ankles hurt. She tried to twist off the bed but her legs felt heavy, leaden, as if restrained. She was powerless to move. She tried to twist her neck, to avert her gaze from the searing heat of the light. The light seemed to follow whichever way she turned. She screwed her eyes as tightly shut as they would go but the light still penetrated, as if it were inside her head. Then the pain came. It was inside her, inside her stomach, right inside her bones.

Natasha vomited. Somewhere inside her she knew this time she would surely choke to death as the viscous fluid blocked her windpipe. She fought the urge to cough, welcoming the final release from this endless torment.

Gently the ties on her wrist were loosened, soft voices directing the hands as they worked calmly but quickly with a sense of urgency, turning her on her side and clearing her airway.

Natasha could smell antiseptic, the faint smell of bleach, clean sheets; smells from a different life, a different time. Soap: the smell of clean skin. Natasha's thoughts drifted to the unique scent of a baby's skin; that brand new smell that only a newborn has. Memories flooded back, overwhelming her. Her eyes snapped open, her head arched back. She could hear voices, voices calling her name, a desperate scream, a scream so loud that it hurt her ears. The scream died in her throat as she felt a sharp pinprick in her arm. Quietly, gently, she drifted back into welcome unconsciousness.

## CHAPTER FORTY SIX

**Arrival**

The plane from Dublin touched down on the warm tarmac of Fort Worth airport. The man alighted from the plane. It was early in the morning; the man was only slightly conspicuous, dressed as he was in warm clothes, ill-suited for the heat of the day to come. Carrying only a rucksack, he was pretty indistinguishable from any number of travel weary back-packers who passed through the airport at the start of some global adventure, or ticking off experiences from a 'bucket list'. As he disembarked immigration unimpeded, a security guard stopped him and asked him what had happened to his hand. He held his left hand up to show angry scar tissue and raw stitches around the missing digit. Speaking in a broad Irish dialect, he laughed, "Sliced me finger clean off with a boning knife so I did. Back home, I'm a butcher so I am." The irony of the exchange was lost on the guard. "Trouble is, I'm a sucker for a drop of the amber nectar too," he smiled, making a drinking motion with his good right hand. "The two seldom mix!"

The security official smiled and beckoned him through with a cheery wave. "Get on through there Mick, and be sure you don't go causing a ruckus while you're here!"

"Just passing through, but I'll be good, to be sure!" Brian Dix assured the man.

His pace quickened as he made for the taxi rank. The early morning cool was already being displaced by the encroaching sun. Brian Dix reached into his inside pocket and withdrew an address. Leaning into the window of the first cab he came to, he asked, "Can you take me to Waco?"

"Waco? Jeez buddy, that's gotta be a good eighty miles, wouldn't you be better hiring yourself a car?"

Brian Dix cursed, "Shit. OK, just take me to the nearest place out of town that I can hire a motor."

"You got it buddy, my brother-in-law's got himself a car lot just outta town. He'll fix you up with a cosy deal." He touched his nose. "Discretion guaranteed, if that's your thing."

Brian looked disinterested. "Mmm, that'll do, take me there."

"First time in the *Lone Star State*, buddy?" the cabbie asked, launching into his practised banter.

Brian interrupted, his voice laced with vitriol, "Can we dispense with the bullshit? I like my peace and quiet, if you know what I mean, *buddy*."

Taken aback by the abrupt rebuttal, the cabbie replied with, "Suit yourself friend, there's no extra charge for rudeness."

Without another word, the cabbie pulled up at the car lot.

"Good luck buddy," the cabbie remarked as Brian handed him the fare, then waited for his change. Obviously not about to receive a tip, the cabbie snapped, "You're gonna need it with your attitude." As he sped away, he stuck his left hand out of the driver's window in a one finger salute, shouting, "Yuh jerk!"

Brian grinned and walked over to the car lot.

The deal done, he wheel-spun the Camaro out of the parking area, eliciting a look of consternation from the salesman.

The guy behind the counter had loaned him a large scale map of the Marble Falls area. He decided not to linger too long at the car lot; best not give them too clear a memory of him, just in case. He pulled to the side of the road before joining the freeway and studied the map.

With the digits on his good right hand he was using his thumb and forefinger to estimate the distance from his present location to a property on the shores of Lake Travis.

He travelled on for about an hour. Clear of the urban sprawl of Fort Worth, Marble Falls was his ultimate destination but he elected to take the I35 towards Waco rather than the more direct route. Waco was the place he was to pick up the provisions he needed. The historical notoriety of the place appealed to Brian's twisted sense of humour. After travelling a few miles Southbound on I35, he pulled off the road and headed into the town of Burleson. Just inside the town boundary, he pulled into a gigantic parking lot; dotted along the edge of the parking lot were a number of popular super-stores. Brian scanned along the stores looking for a name he recognised.

He parked up, locked the Camaro and hurried across to the Radio Shack store. Half an hour later he exited the shop carrying a pair of powerful 'Citizens Band' radios and a bag containing numerous electrical components, batteries, solder and a soldering iron.

Throwing his purchases onto the passenger seat, Brian fired up the car and drove out of the lot in the direction of the town. He hadn't travelled more than a hundred yards when the motel sign beckoned. The reception office was a good indication of what could be expected from the rooms. Splintered wood panels hung from the walls, held in place by years of viscous nicotine and memory. Dancing erratic circles on the cracked plaster of the ceiling, like a decrepit fairground waltzer, hung a filthy fan, whose remaining blades numbered exactly the amount of crusty decayed teeth in the mouth of the receptionist; a man old beyond his years who was meticulously studying a dog-eared smut mag.

Brian walked up to the customer's side of the counter. The gnarly old man looked at him, but not a word was spoken. The bell sat on the cluttered desk a few inches below the man's chin. Brian looked the man straight in the eyes and hit the ringer as hard as the limited space would allow.

"Ay-hole," the old man cursed.

"I want a room for a couple of nights," Brian demanded, pulling a wad of notes from his pocket.

"Fifty bucks. No whores in the rooms, no drinking and no goddamn hoe-moe-sexuals," the old geezer spat.

"I'll be moving on tomorrow, but I want to wake up naturally so I'll pay you for two nights, understand?"

"Fifty bucks. In advance. And no funny business in the room," the old man reiterated. "Did ya hear what I said boy?"

"I am too tired for whores, thank you for the offer, and I have no plans to become a homosexual anytime soon so be sure my friend, your arse is safe from me!"

"Everyone's a fucking co-me-dien!" The old man cursed. "That or a mother-fucking, whore luvin', son of a bitch, hoe-moe-sexual."

Brian handed him the wad of notes and the old man tossed him a key fastened to a block of wood the size of a coffee cup.

"Room fifteen, straight across the yard, on the left." With that, the old man went back to staring at his girly mag, as if Brian didn't exist.

Brian opened the room. Tossing his purchases on the night stand, he threw back the grubby covers and lay straight down on the bed shutting his eyes. First, he needed to sleep off the jet-lag. In the morning he would require a clear head and a power supply to fabricate his own unique insurance policy.

## CHAPTER FORTY SEVEN

**Absent mind**

"How is she doing Doctor?" Neil asked.

"She is a fighter Neil, she is coming back faster than we expected." He examined his notes as if preparing for a speech. "She is exhibiting good cognitive signs. After such a huge overdose, and considering the skull fracture, it's not uncommon for patients to suffer from a degree of 'locked in syndrome' not unlike a stroke victim. We have your wife heavily sedated for her own comfort while she fights the worst of the withdrawal. She is drifting in and out of consciousness, but nevertheless, when she is with us, she seems quite responsive as if she is aware of her surroundings. As soon as we believe it safe to do so, we would like to reduce the level of sedation and allow her to come back to full consciousness so that we can assess the level of cognitive recovery."

"So is the prognosis looking promising?" Neil asked.

"At this stage Neil, I would say we have good reason for optimism. We were not expecting this degree of cognitive awareness, especially considering the level of sedation. I believe it's a sure sign that Natasha is fighting back, trying to take back control. It's my belief that the best course of action is to gently bring her back to Earth and see how she copes."

"What exactly do you have in mind?" Neil questioned, puzzled.

"It's a bit radical Neil, but I suggest we keep her sympathetically restrained to minimise her ability to cause herself harm, then reduce the sedation and bring her back to full consciousness."

"Sympathetically restrain her. What exactly does that mean? Are you thinking like, a straitjacket?" Neil was clearly not comfortable with the suggestion.

"No Neil, this isn't a sanatorium, Natasha is not a prisoner here. What I am suggesting is that she be supervised by nursing staff twenty-four seven. I would also like to keep her arms and legs restrained, just until she begins to awaken, then we can remove the restraints before she even becomes aware of their existence. It's just a safeguard to prevent her coming around abruptly and harming herself. It's a necessary precaution."

"I am really not keen that she wake up and find herself shackled. After what she's been through, that's the last shock she needs," Neil confessed.

"Neil, please, trust me. We know what is best for her," the doctor reassured. "Right now that is for us to make sure she doesn't do herself any harm until she has had the opportunity to become fully conscious and aware of her new situation."

"OK Doc, you are the professional, whatever you think is best has my support," Neil concluded

## CHAPTER FORTY EIGHT

**Diablo cometh**

Brian slept like a baby. By early afternoon he had caught up on his sleep and managed to fabricate a few high tech gadgets from his bag of components. Now he was ready for the next leg of his trip.

Back out on route, he drove on for an hour or so, leaving the urban sprawl behind, before a need for food convinced him to pull off the highway and filter in between the wagons and pick-up trucks sharing the spacious car park in front of a predictably gaudy roadhouse.

Shouldering his way between the baseball caps and lumberjack shirts, Brian caught the attention of the big- breasted bottle-blonde behind the bar. Dressed in a 'Hooter's' style uniform of tied off shirt, bare midriff, no bra and a skirt she grew out of back in high school, she was clearly employed to attract the punters, not for her bar-keeping skills.

"Howdy stranger!" she called out, the disinterested expression instantly disguised behind a pouting façade of practised sexuality. It was her task to keep the regulars travelling out of town drinking there, and to keep discerning truckers using the gas station to fill up.

"Hi," Brian replied, "can I be getting some change to use yer phone?"

"Hey," the blonde exclaimed, now with genuine interest, "are you from London, England?"

"No," Brian spat. "I'm not from fecking London England. Now can I just get some change for the phone?"

The blonde looked deflated; anger welled up inside her at the rude response she'd received for her courtesy. "The phone's for customers only." She made to turn away from Brian but he caught her wrist. Only now did she really look at the man; the apparent depth of evil in his eyes sent an instant shiver up her spine. She looked furtively in the direction of the entrance to where the highway patrol normally kept a regular table. Today, the table was empty.

Releasing her hand, Brian's tone softened to a warm Irish brogue as he said, "I'll have a beer then please, pretty lady." Brian could turn on the Irish charm when the moment warranted it and he didn't need any trouble here. "I'm an Irishman, so I am; we're not known to be friends of the English."

"Oh God, I'm so sorry," the girl replied, her body relaxing as the therapeutic effect of the compliment washed the tension away. "I'm such a klutz; I don't recognise accents too well."

"I've been accused of being Scottish before, but never English. No harm done though darling. Now, how about that phone?"

She smiled and pulled Brian a glass of weak branded beer. "That'll be two bucks please," she purred.

Brian handed her a ten dollar bill. "Here you go, get yourself one and give me the rest in quarters for the phone."

"Why thank you sir, I do believe I may have a soft spot for Irishmen!"

Brian smiled, took his change and his beer and made for the pay-phone. He pulled a scrap of paper from his wallet and made a call.

After just two rings the call was answered. The person on the receiving end took a long pull on a cigarette before speaking. The gravelly voice said, "Donovan's!"

"Is Brodie there?" Brian enquired.

"Who wants to know?" the voice questioned.

"The Irishman."

A pause, followed by, "I'll see if he's out back."

As the noise of the phone being put down on the bar died away, Brian could just about make out shouts above the noise of a Harley Davidson revving up in an enclosed building.

"*Brodie!*" Brian heard shouted above the din.

The revving was cut short. "Brodie, your call, the Irishman."

After a time, there was a crackle on the line as the receiver was picked up. "Brodie," the man affirmed.

"Brodie, the name's Brian Dix, you've got some toys fer me?"

"Yea, Irish. We'll sort out your shopping list, when will you be dropping by?"

"I'm about an hour off. Have you got what I need there?"

"No way buddy, we didn't know for sure you would be coming. I'll need a couple of days to fill your list. Come on over to the club house and we'll put on a party; show you a good time while you wait. It's the least we can do for our Irish cousins."

"I've got a bit of business first, be there in a few hours!"

"Looking forward to meeting you Irish! What are you driving? You know where to find us?"

"Blue 89 Camaro. Donovan's, Route 133 South, right?" Brian offered.

"Near enough Irish, just follow the Harleys!" Brodie hung up.

Brian strolled back into the diner. With a couple of hours to kill and the promise of a good party, he decided to have a punt on Blondie!

Pulling up a bar stool, he called across to her, "Hey gorgeous, what you recommend for a hungry Irishman with money to spend?"

Bottle-blonde sashayed across to his side of the bar and drew his attention to the name-tag pinned to her ample, half exposed breast. "Tammy," she said, "but you'll have to wait till I get off at ten. In the meantime, the side of ribs will keep your motor runnin'."

Brian Dix smiled; he still had it. It was like shooting fish in a barrel!

Just after ten, Tammy threw her apron on the pile of beer crates in the doorway and slipped out of the screen door.

Brian met her outside.

"We can't go to my place, my old man will bust a vein. You got somewhere to go?" she asked.

"Yea, I've got somewhere to be an hour or so down the road, it's a party; somewhere to crash for a day or two."

"Sounds like a blast," she said. "Let's go before my ride turns up."

As they came upon the outskirts of Waco, two chopped Harley Davidsons pulled alongside, flanking them. Both riders were sporting leather cut-off jackets and wrap-around shades despite the absence of natural light. On their cut-offs they wore badges known as 'bottom rockers' spelling out the word 'Waco'. The absence of 'top rockers' or 'centre-pieces' described the role of these men within their club hierarchy; they were 'prospects' – prospective members who had not yet earned the right to be 'full patch' members.

Brian wound the window down.

The biker on Brian's side, a huge tattooed Native American, turned his expressionless face towards the car window and said, "Irish?"

Brian nodded. The two bikes pulled in front before leaving the highway at the next junction. The tarmac ended abruptly and they were on a shale/cinder track which wound its way through the barren vista.

Eventually, they came into a valley. Dominating the scene stood a huge roadhouse service station with bar and workshop attached. The car-park was filled with every imaginable design of chopped Harley from café-racer sportsters, pans, ratty shovels, flat tracker XRs to low riders, representing every model produced by the Milwaukee marque. Above the door was a neon sign. Only half the letters were illuminated but you could see it *should* have read 'Donovan's'.

As they came to a halt, Brodie, a huge tattooed, bearded, mountain of a man, wrenched the Camaro door open. Practically lifting Brian from the driver's seat, he grasped his right hand in a classic biker thumb grab handshake.

"Welcome brother! Who's the chick? Your old lady?"

"No," Brian replied, "just picked her up in a diner an hour up the road!"

"Good man Irish, I like a man who brings his own candy to a party!"

Brodie turned to Tammy. "Girl, go get us a couple beers and get yourself fixed up with some gear. We got everything; white lines, acid, whatever your heart desires to make the party go with a bang!"

A little apprehensive at the sight of all the tattooed outlaw bikers, Tammy's eyes lit up at the prospect of a line of coke. On her meagre wages from the diner, and with a drunken sot of a husband to support, she didn't get too many offers to snort coke. She trotted off obediently.

The two men followed Tammy inside the diner.

With her out of earshot, Brodie lowered his voice and said, "If that don't work out man, anything you see not sat on a knee is a 'loaner', just tell 'em what you want and they'll oblige." He turned to a pair of scrawny young girls playing pool. "Hey Cindy, get over here!" The girl obligingly sauntered over. If cleanliness were next to godliness, this girl was no churchgoer.

Brodie caught hold of her left breast and lifted it out of her bodice. "Cindy here's only got small tits but she can suck start a jumbo jet!" As he let go of her, she blew him a kiss and went back to her game.

## CHAPTER FORTY NINE

**Outlaw creed**

The bikers all wore their cut offs, proclaiming devout loyalty to their outlaw biker cult. Brian had no interest in their allegiance; they were associates. Their main source of income was from the sale of illegal drugs. They laundered their drug money through the coffers of Nor-Relief, the charity which raised money stateside for the victims of violence in Northern Ireland, known to be a front for the PIRA. In return, they acted as enforcers on behalf of the Provo's stateside, and with a little gentle extortion helped to ensure Irish ex-pats remained generous and the Nor-Relief money kept flowing. To Brian, there were only two things which worked in his world, power and fear; he was loyal to those who protected him and to those he feared. His men remained loyal to him for the same reasons. To Brian, his Provisional IRA masters and these outlaws were just fools to a cause. Not him. Power, and the rush that it brought, the fear he saw in his enemy's eyes, that was the only cause worth fighting for. He glanced towards his mutilated hand; everything else was just survival.

On Tammy's return, Brodie chugged his beer in one hit then turned to Brian and said, "Hey man, don't take it personally, but I gotta light out and score some of your goodies. Just remember, you're among friends here, you just relax and have yourself a time. There's bunks out back; couple with double beds." Brodie winked and gestured towards Tammy. "If the mood takes you.

Anything behind the bar or in the coolers is free to help yourself. You need anything to eat, just ask one of the old ladies and they'll rustle something up. We got a meat locker out back with provisions for a month, so don't go crashing with a hungry belly. I'll catch up with you in the morning."

With that, Brodie took his leave and roared away up the road.

## CHAPTER FIFTY

**Party girl**

Brian took a long look at Tammy; she looked pretty tidy for his first pull on American soil. In comparison, the 'loaner' biker girls were a rough, unkempt bunch. They would do if push came to shove but only if he struck out with Tammy.

There wasn't much chance of that!

"Hey baby," she purred, traces of white powder clinging to the soft moist skin of her upper lip. "Are we gonna party or what?"

"Aye, we're going to party!" Brian promised.

The first door he opened revealed a huge double bed covered with animal skins; weird, but fine for Brian's purposes.

Tammy dropped onto the bed, untying the knot in her shirt and letting her full breasts spill into view. In contrast to her pale skin she had large, cherry red nipples. Brian suspected that the bottle-blonde was disguising a natural red-head. His suspicions were confirmed as the skirt and knickers followed the shirt.

She dropped to her knees like a pro, and soon had Brian's trousers and undies round his ankles. His limp manhood was quickly swallowed up between those juicy red lips. Within a second, Tammy was sucking him for all she was worth.

Not used to a woman taking the initiative, Brian was lagging behind.

"C'mon baby, get it up," Tammy crooned, sucking him harder. "C'mon baby, I need fucking real bad, don't you go disappointing me now."

## Bittersweet Humiliation

Brian was outside of his comfort zone; his manhood, his very virility, was letting him down. His head was reeling; the fucking wog threatening him, his IRA masters betraying him, his mutilated hand. "That fucking bitch Natasha," he shouted. "I'll fucking kill that bitch slow when I catch up to her."

"Whoa baby," Tammy exclaimed, ejecting Brian's semi erect penis from her mouth. "What's your problem honey, you don't like girls huh?"

The stone ashtray on the bedside locker was the first thing that came to hand; Brian swung it at the unfortunate girl's head with ample force to smash a coconut. The first blow was enough to start a fatal chain reaction in the girl's skull, but the second blow was just for fun. Now Brian could achieve a complete erection. He graphically demonstrated his ability to complete the sex act as the life oozed from her shattered skull.

"Now you're fucked baby, now you're really fucked, so you are. You won't get fucked like this again, not in this life!"

As he reached his climax Brian screamed out, "BITCH!"

As his penis returned to its flaccid state he stared into Tammy's lifeless eyes, kissed her on the lips and said, "Thanks baby! That was just grrrrrreat! Hope it was good for you too!"

As the heat of the evening gave way to the cold kiss of night the lifeless body on the bed next to him began to cool by degrees. He knew nothing about her. Was she a mother, did she have aspirations of having children, was she loved, did she love someone? Brian couldn't care less; he had a job to do.

He slipped out of the bed and got dressed into his pants. Creeping out into the clubhouse, he was pleased to see that the earlier drinking and drug fuelled debauchery had led to a general condition of coma amongst the remaining revelers.

He quietly crept out to the Camaro and retrieved his bag of toys, which he had manufactured the night before.

Back in the clubhouse, Brian picked up the receiver behind the bar. There was no dial tone. *Damn,* he thought. No dial tone meant that this was only an extension; the main phone must be elsewhere. Following the phone line it was evident that the main phone was in Brodie's little office, off the workshop. As luck would have it, the door wasn't locked.

He let himself in and then proceeded to fit his home made device into the body of Brodie's phone.

Returning, smug from the success of his little side mission, Brian's confidence was returning and with it his libido.

Sliding back between the covers, he stroked his fingers across Tammy's breasts. She still retained a little residual body heat.

"Warm enough," Brian thought aloud as he parted her lifeless legs and began to indulge in the most brutal act of inhumanity short of cannibalism.

# CHAPTER FIFTY ONE

## Necrophilia

Brian was preparing breakfast for himself when Brodie walked in.

"Hey buddy, sleep well? All partied out? Where's the squeeze, sleeping it off I'd guess huh?"

"Oh aye, I dare say she'll be sleeping a while yet. Sleeping the big sleep you might say," he replied with a degree of irony.

"Good for you Irish, wore the bitch out huh?" Brodie enquired in high spirits.

"Aye, I think I wore her out completely. May need to swap her out for a new model."

"Good man, good for you. Just as long as you enjoyed yourself. Now then, onto business."

A scream shattered the quiet atmosphere of the morning. Brodie recognised the screamer as one of the 'ole ladies' who took care of business around the clubhouse and immediately went to investigate.

"What the fuck? What in the name of God has gone on here?" Brodie rushed back into the bar and grabbed Brian by the throat. "What the fuck man, why is there a dead girl in the bed with her goddamn head stoved in?"

"We had a difference of opinion," Brian offered.

"What the hell does that mean? You've smashed her goddamn skull in. Jesus Christ, what the fuck?"

Brodie stood with a hand to his temple, clearly trying to get a handle on Brian. "Why did you kill her man?"

"She served her purpose!" Brian answered.

"You fucking psycho," Brodie shouted. "I want you out of our clubhouse." Brodie hurried out into the yard and summoned the prospects who had escorted Brian in the night before. They were busy carrying beer in to replenish the bar stocks. Pulling a revolver from his waistband, Brodie handed the pistol to the bigger of the two men and commanded, "You two keep an eye on this mad dog. If he moves a fucking muscle, shoot him square between the eyes."

Brodie strode over to the office and angrily stamped at the dial pad on the office phone.

"Yeah, it's Brodie, Waco Slaves. Can I speak with Mr Doherty?" After a short wait the receiver was picked up by the appropriate recipient.

"Doherty!"

"Mr Doherty, it's Brodie from the Waco Slaves over in the States."

"Hello Mr Brodie, I trust you are affording our man every courtesy?"

"Mr Doherty, your man's gone psycho. He brought a woman here, a civilian. He smashed her skull in last night with a goddamn ashtray!"

There was a pause as the man in Ireland digested this information. Doherty had gone out on a limb for Brian Dix. There were many in the army who elected to slit his throat after the unfortunate incident at Cherry Tree Farm, where Brian Dix had led a number of their ranks into a primed ambush instead of the 'soft target' they were expecting. Brian's allies were fast losing faith.

"Mr Brodie, can you contain the unfortunate incident?"

"Yes I can, Mr Doherty, but I will need your man gone, he's gonna be as hot as a chili dog when the bitch is missed."

"Could you put our Mr Dix on the phone for me please Mr Brodie, would you be so kind?" the voice at the end of the receiver requested.

"Just a minute," Brodie answered, and then returned with Brian Dix.

"Your boss wants a word," he spat, handing Brian the phone.

"Mr Dix, why have you fucked up and made me look a fool again? Are you determined to embarrass me in front of our American cousins who go out of their way to afford you every courtesy?"

"Sorry Mr Doherty, the girl pissed me off. It won't affect the job," Brian answered, his arrogant attitude vanquished.

"It had better not Mr Dix. We have an address for your 'client'. she is enjoying a stay in a cuckoo's nest not far from the address you were heading for."

"A cuckoo's nest?" Brian enquired, confused.

"A nuthouse Brian, a loony bin. What do the Americans call it? Rehab. Now be a good fellow Brian and get a pen and paper, I'll give you the address."

Brian gestured to Brodie for a pen and paper. Brodie reluctantly complied, handing him a pen and a beer mat.

Their business concluded, Doherty asked to be passed back to Brodie.

"Do you feel able to conclude our agreed business with Mr Dix, Mr Brodie?"

"I've got half the stuff he wanted, I was waiting on the rest of his requirements. It's too great a risk, letting him stay here now." Brodie was planning as he spoke. "I'll have to send him on to some of our associates."

"Mr Brodie, I understand your predicament, but we would be grateful if you could help us to facilitate getting Mr Dix's assignment concluded."

"I'll send him off to an associate MC in Brady where he can bed-down with some boys we use as mules. It won't be the lap of luxury but it will keep him out of our way and hopefully out of trouble," Brodie mused.

"We're indebted to you Mr Brodie! We will take care of our errant Mr Dix when his business has been resolved."

As Brodie put the phone down, Doherty had already decided: as soon as this job was completed, he would terminate Brian Dix's services. His mental instability made him a loose cannon. If the client hadn't insisted on Brian taking care of the job, they would have severed something more substantial than his index finger.

Brodie kicked open the clubhouse door. He strode back through the bar, back to the bedside of the dead woman. Brodie had a secret weakness; he loved women. It wasn't just that he loved having *sex* with women, he really loved them, worshipped them at an almost spiritual level. In his position it was a given that he would exploit and use women. The outlaw biker world was a real *'man's world'*. This attitude never sat well with Brodie; he couldn't help but respect women and it was an effort to keep up the façade. This incident pushed him to the limits. The girl had been beautiful. She was perfect – perfect body, perfect pretty face. She had struck him as a pleasant person too. He hated Brian Dix for doing this, hated him with every nerve and fiber of his body.

As Brian had exited the bed, he had pulled the covers from the girl's cold body. Brodie looked at her still form; his eyes were drawn to the shiny pearls matting the girl's pubic hair and the yellowy stain on the bed sheet immediately below her sex. In an instant, he realised that Brian had desecrated her lifeless form.

"Mother fucker!" he shrieked. "Son of a mother fucking bitch!"

In an attempt to restore the unfortunate girl's dignity he covered her naked body and smashed features with the animal skins.

Brodie drew himself up to his full six foot four. Staring down into Brian Dix's cold, callous eyes he said, "You're a fucking mental case man! If I had it my way, I'd snap your neck for you right now!" He turned away from Brian Dix's smug stare. "I have to help you do whatever it is you're here to do! I don't like it and I don't like you. As far as I'm concerned, you've burned your Waco privileges. We'll take care of the mess you've made here, but I want you out of my clubhouse now. I'll arrange for you to bed down with some associates of ours in McCulloch County. It's no luxury hotel but it's better than you deserve. The boys over at Brady MC are wild; most of them are using more product than they're selling. Don't fuck with them otherwise you will wind up dead." He barked his orders to the two prospects.

## Bittersweet Humiliation

As they escorted Brian Dix to his hire car, he called back to Brodie, "Hey Brodie, you didn't miss much, she was a lousy fuck, just lay there like a fucking corpse! You seem to have a hard-on for her, have a go; you'll see what I mean!" He spun the wheels of the Camaro as he left the roadhouse, falling in behind his escort on their bikes. His mocking laughter drifted away down the valley.

Brodie cursed out loud. "You and me my friend have a date with destiny."

## CHAPTER FIFTY TWO

**The job**

Brian was regretting the impulsive killing of Tammy. Not out of any feelings of guilt or remorse, but just because the conditions in Brady were harsh. Unlike the MC in Waco, these boys were all mentalists. Their clubhouse was a wild frontier. Brian was having problems getting any sleep; besides the flea infestation, there was the insistence of every club member to rev their Harleys to the throttle stop all through the night and then, when they were too drunk to keep going, start discharging firearms until the ammo ran out or someone got shot. Brian Dix decided to move out in the morning and get the job done, with or without his complete shopping list. Life here was more dangerous than back in Belfast.

He was truly suffering in the Texan heat. It was only a few days since he had left the cold wet climate of Ireland. The temperature difference was a killer. He had been parked up outside the Spirit Lodge Rehab Centre in Meadowlakes, near Marble Falls, for a whole morning. Without functioning air conditioning the temperature in the dark Camaro was soaring. He had spotted a potential flaw in the center's security already; the private ambulance entrance. Patients were constantly transferred between clinics and the center, and the ambulances were little more than glorified taxis. As far as Brian could see, security weren't scrutinising the ID of every driver, intern or orderly who travelled in or out of the center. This was the weak link; his way in.

Brian cursed; he could see no alternative for what he had planned than to enlist the help of a couple of his new found associates from the Brady MC. This unknown quantity would make the job a lot more risky. He knew it was no use speaking to Brodie, he had burned his bridges there.

Back at Brady, Brian approached the biker who called himself Zack. He appeared the leader of this motley crew, if there were such a thing in this group.

"Zack, listen chap, I'm going to need a couple of your guys to help me out with the job I've got on. Can you spare me a couple of your guys, preferably not knuckle draggers? Do ye have a couple of blokes that look normal?"

"What the hell is a bloke?" Zack replied, snorting the white powder residue from his moustache.

"Jesus, Mary and Joseph," Brian cursed. "D'ye have any guys who have a job of work at all, couple of tidy guys who I can pass off as hospital workers, orderlies?"

"Hey," Zack replied, "I ain't here to wipe your ass, I just gotta make sure you keep breathing. You wanna be my friend, let's see the colour of your money, then we can be friends. Hell, I may even let you suck my dick!"

"OK Zack, I need a couple of tidy guys, beards trimmed, hair tied back and I need them clean and sober. What's that going to cost me?" Brian asked, defeated.

Zack smiled. "That's better buddy, show respect for the cut. You don't talk to me like a goddamn hoe, less you wants your fucking tongue cutting out!"

The man was clearly pissed, high, mental or all of the above; a winning combination.

"You can have a couple of prospects. We got a couple of real fucking straights, probably won't make the cut but they're loyal, they'll do as they're told. Cost you five hundred apiece, in advance!"

Brian had picked up his Western Union wire transfer in town earlier so money wasn't a problem. He counted out the thousand dollars to Zack.

"And the sundries," Zack commanded.

"What?"

"Two hundred dollars, for sundries." He insisted, "There's always sundries buddy, otherwise known as misc, or should that be a charge for sundries and an extra charge for misc?"

Brian handed him a further two hundred dollars and cautioned, "That's yer lot buddy, now it's you who's doing the disrespecting!"

Zack laughed, "OK my funny little Irish friend, now you sure you won't suck my dick?"

Brian glared at him. Despite his intoxication, Zack sensed the joke had played out and summoned the two least offensive looking prospects.

"You two, whatever Irish here wants, you see to it he gets it!"

The two men nodded.

"You got 'em for two days Irish, I give you a day out of the kindness of my heart. Be sure to get done what it is you have to do before I get tired of being your fucking nursemaid and cut your fucking heart out. Just you know this: I don't jump for that dumb fuck Brodie and I sure as hell don't jump for you!"

## Bittersweet Humiliation

There wouldn't be time for planning; they'd have to fly by the seat of their pants. It took about an hour but Brian had his two prospects looking like gorillas who'd been put in suits and strategically shaved. They were as ready as they would ever be.

Brian instructed his two pawns to get to bed early, no alcohol and to avoid getting shot through the night; it would be an early start in the morning.

## CHAPTER FIFTY THREE

**Callous**

Up with the rising sun, Brian and his two aides were cruising Tenth Street, Marble Falls. Brian had the idea to find a suitable secluded parking garage and then phone for an ambulance to come there. He planned to overpower the crew and steal the truck and ID passes. As luck would have it, they fell in behind a private ambulance. Reluctant to pass up an opportunity, Brian tailed the truck discretely. He couldn't believe his luck when the truck pulled into an underground parking garage beneath a deserted funeral home.

The three man crew were surprised and easily overpowered. Brian and his stooges dragged the protesting men to the corner of the parking garage, an area littered with discarded cardboard boxes and huge metal dumpsters.

The prospects were busy removing the men's belts and attempting to restrain their arms.

"What are you doing?" Brian asked.

"Tying them up," one of the prospects replied. "Stop them getting away!"

Brian pulled the black metal pistol from his belt; he fired twice. Two of the crewmen fell. "There you go, they're not getting away! Stick 'em in the skip," he instructed, gesturing with the gun towards the dumpster.

Dragging the remaining terrified crewman back into the ambulance, he instructed, "You got anaesthetic, morphine and the like in here? Mix yourself up a cocktail that'll see you unconscious and you will live to see another day. When you wake up, I'll be gone and you'll be alive. Fuck me around or try to fool me and you join your friends on the dumpster ride, is that clear?"

The crewman nodded and did as he was told. When he had finished preparing the hypodermic, Brian instructed him to inject himself and lie down on the ambulance gurney. After seeing his colleagues callously butchered, he was in no mood to argue and he followed Brian's instructions.

The plan went off like clockwork and within minutes of arriving at the clinic, Brian was inside.

Making straight for reception, Brian appeared panicked as he announced, "Quickly, someone help us, this patient has suffered a seizure on the way over. We're not medically trained. We're just porters!"

The receptionist; a young trainee nurse, hit the crash team button and in the ensuing melee Brian liberated the room plan from the reception desk and was in the first elevator he came to, frantically scouring the plan for Natasha's details.

## CHAPTER FIFTY FOUR

**When worlds collide**

Natasha was inside the womb, swimming, caught up in the current of a vortex pulling her down. Harder and harder she thrashed against the dry, torturous sand which held her trapped, running back, filling every trench she carved, covering every avenue of escape her flailing limbs created. Slowly, the sand melted away to oil, viscous black treacle which caused her arms to ache with the sheer weight of movement. Slowly, surely, she made progress and the oil thinned to water. The current returned but it was water, now she knew what to do, how to escape its clutches. She held her breath and thrashed with all her might towards the surface. Her lungs straining at bursting point, she broke the surface. Her first sweet breath of freedom. Consciousness brought comprehension flooding back; memory of a lifetime forgotten. Her whole body arched against the restraints on her wrists and ankles before the sheer exhaustion of the exertion on her wasted muscles set her body crashing back down onto the hospital bed.

Her eyes were open, her pupils focused. For a fraction of a second, Natasha had been fully conscious. Her eyes sent an instant snapshot of her surroundings to her brain. In that same split second, her brain had processed what it had seen – the evil face of Brian Dix, his knee pressed firmly into the back of the seated nurse. Around her neck he held a shiny length of wire. Blood flowed in an endless torrent over the crisp collar of her white uniform. Her eyes bulged, the life ebbing from them fast.

Natasha pulled her exhausted limbs hard against the restraints in a futile attempt to free herself, to run from this outrageous reality.

Through the fixed stare of her eyes, she could see the scene develop as if through a tunnel; the image grew weaker and ever more distant as her mind took control of her fear and backed into a distant corner of her brain, somewhere she could be away from Brian, somewhere safe.

Down at reception, seeing their deception beginning to unravel, one of the two prospects had taken fright and run out of the door, followed closely by his colleague. Within moments, the observant receptionist noticed the missing room plan and hit the emergency button. Security guards quickly flooded the foyer. The receptionist shouted, "There, two men running towards that ambulance." Before she could warn them that there had been a third man, the guards were chasing out of the door after the two fleeing bikers.

With the sounding of the alarm a security guard began to scour the CCTV monitors. Quickly spotting Brian in Natasha's room he passed the information to the security detail. All messages were patched through to the desk intercom by default. "We have an intruder in room 321, we need armed response quickly!"

The nervous receptionist; showing a resourcefulness way above her pay grade, realised that she had been inadvertently thrust into the role of incident manager, and quickly stabbed the relevant button on the intercom system. "Security, your detail is off the premises chasing two men dressed as orderlies, you'll have to go after the one in room 321 yourself; quickly!"

"Damn," Brian cursed as the wailing sirens alerted him that his cover was blown. Throwing down the garrote he dug into his waistband for the gun, cursing as the thick barrel and forward sight got caught up in his undergarments.

Wrenching the weapon free of its cloth prison, he levelled the sight at Natasha's head.

With dying loyalty to the welfare of her patient, the mortally wounded nurse swung the heavy Sharps peddle bin at Brian's gun hand. Seeing the approaching missile, he swung his empty left hand round to protect himself. The heavy stainless steel bin contacted with his injured hand, dissipating some of its energy before following through, crashing into the side of his head, sending him off balance. Instinctively Brian reached out with his gun hand as the weight of his body sent him sprawling to the floor. The weapon, still carrying the momentum of the fall, flew free of his grasp and skidded across the polished floor out into the hallway. Brian struggled to his feet and lurched into the corridor to retrieve the weapon.

Instinctively, before leaving his post, the guard in the CCTV room hit the button to electronically lock all the patients' rooms.

Outside room 321, the door to the hallway drifted shut, Brian Dix heard the click of the Servo bolts as the security latch responded to the lock-down response. "Damn," he cursed out loud. The shouts of the approaching guard were getting closer. Now the mission was aborted. The new priority: escape!

## CHAPTER FIFTY FIVE

**Escape**

Down on the ground floor, a deputy from the local Sheriff's office had been alerted by the alarms and had rushed into the building. Running straight up to the reception desk he asked, "What's the commotion, why are the alarms sounding?"

The hysterical receptionist brought him up to speed. "There are intruders, they came in with a patient. Two of them have run off but one went up in the lift to the sixth floor."

The seasoned cop glanced over where she was pointing, hesitated, then gestured to the lifts. "You have another elevator, staff only?"

"Yes, just off the stairwell," she replied, grasping the key under the lip of the reception counter. "Here, please hurry; we have a high security patient on the sixth floor, room 321, right out of the elevator, last room on the left." She shouted after him, "One of the security guards has gone after him."

The elevators were designed to fit hospital beds and the two piece door opened completely, leaving nowhere to hide inside the metal box. The streetwise cop was hoping that the less conspicuous service elevator would at least give him the advantage of being able to prepare for this vulnerability, and had drawn his revolver in readiness. Unfortunately, he was momentarily confused trying to remember which way the girl had said to turn as the door slid back. That was all the hesitation Brian Dix needed. Alerted by the hiss of the air rams, which opened the double doors, Brian dropped the cop instantly with two bullets; one to the head and one in the chest.

He leapt over the prostrate Deputy and dragged the dead man back into the lift with him. Thinking on his feet, the natural street cunning of this terrorist for hire was coming into its own.

He punched the stop button as the lift began to move down, jamming it between floors.

As the lift arrived back at the ground floor, the returning security detail, waiting with revolvers drawn at the entrance, were greeted to the spectacle of the Deputy staggering from the elevator, blood spewing from a gruesome hand wound screaming, "He's shot my finger off, the bastard's shot my finger off." As a medic rushed over to help him, the Deputy shouted to the guards, "The one in the elevator's dead but there are two more on the sixth floor, they've got a patient hostage." He gestured with his mangled hand to cement the point. "Get up there and keep them pinned down, I'll call for backup!" As they dragged the dead body clear of the lift, the Deputy advised them, "Go up to the seventh floor and use the stairs. The lift is a death trap, there's no cover."

Grateful of the advice and with absolutely no doubt of his sincerity, the security detail took off in the elevator quickly ascending floors and out of earshot of the reception.

The receptionist was staring at the dead body on the floor; recognition and comprehension were making their way through retina and optic nerve. The process took no longer than it took to blink. She had seen the dead man only minutes before and he had been wearing a deputy's badge. She heard the crack of the regulation sidearm. Turning as if in slow motion she saw the medic drop. Another flash of the muzzle, a further retort, and a dull thud sent her flying back into her seat. Out of the corner of her eye she could see the medic who was a colleague, her friend, lying on the cold stone floor; a crimson stain was seeping out around where he lay. It occurred to her that she had never felt such a heavy weight resting against her chest before. Another dull thud kicked the residual breath from her lungs and she stopped thinking.

Running from the building Brian was cursing his injured hand; it hurt like hell. It was the most desperate thing he had ever done, shooting off the stump like that, but it had worked; he was free!

He ran the first few blocks before ducking into an alleyway and tucking his injured hand into his pocket. He continued on at a more sedate pace, not wishing to draw attention to himself. A running cop would be bound to draw attention in a one horse town like Marble Falls.

Reaching the side street where he had stashed the Camaro earlier, Brian was relieved to find it still there.

Quickly stripping down to his tee shirt, he threw the blood soaked police uniform under the nearest car and sped off in the direction of Brady and comparative safety.

# CHAPTER FIFTY SIX

**Persona non grata**

"Looking at you, I don't need to ask if you won," Zack commented, staring at Brian's bloody hand. "Where the hell are my prospects?"

"The bastard cowards cleared out as soon as we encountered trouble," Brian spat.

"Ah well, I said they wouldn't make the cut. So where are they now, jail?" Zack questioned.

"No idea," Brian replied honestly.

"So what now?" Zack asked.

"I missed the fucking mark. I guess I'll have to stick around till things quiet down, then have another shot."

"Not here you won't buddy, you've outstayed your welcome. I'm afraid it's time you were moving on," Zack advised.

"Look, if it's a question of money," Brian protested.

"It ain't a question of money amigo, your money's no good here no more. I just want you gone Irish. Get your stuff and then get the hell out of my clubhouse."

Brian could see he was running out of options.

## CHAPTER FIFTY SEVEN

### Looking after number one

Warren had just finished a speakerphone call with Spirit Lodge.

"Jesus Christ Neil, we nearly lost her again!"

Neil screamed, "What's the matter with that evil bastard, why can't he just leave us alone?"

"I've arranged with the clinic to call in a private security team Neil; they'll surround her 24/7 until we can bring her here. He won't get another crack at her, I promise you."

Neil grabbed the keys to Nell's sedan.

"OK if I use the sedan Warren?" Neil asked, urgency and stress in his voice. "I'm going across to the clinic, see how she's doing. The poor mare, the shock of this is going to knock her right back."

"I'll drive you Neil, if that's OK, you didn't ought to be alone and I want to see her too, reassure her we're on the case, that this won't happen again."

"Christ Warren, how the hell does he do it, waltz right into a secure facility and start killing people?"

"I don't know Neil, but I know one thing – after killing a deputy he's going to find Texas a pretty hostile place. There ain't going to be many places for Mr Brian Dix to hide from a vengeful Sheriff's office."

"Best we make a move Warren. I need to make sure she's OK!"

The clinic was a crime scene. Warren's notoriety got them through the gates but getting into the building would take a little more effort. As luck would have it, Dr Ward was stood in the reception area as Neil and Warren arrived. She spoke to the officer in charge and Neil and Warren were waved through to a small white marquee where they were given white suits, paper shoes and white paper masks to wear.

"Please, don't touch anything gentlemen," the officer in charge said. "I appreciate that this is a working clinic, but it's an active crime scene first and foremost."

Dr Ward waved the two men into a makeshift office.

"Neil, thank you for coming straight over," she said.

"How's my wife Doctor?" Neil asked, his voice barely masking the anxiety he felt.

"Neil, this further shock to her system has left Natasha in a minimal responsive state. She has withdrawn into herself. We have had to sedate her again. She has had a full MRI scan to rule out any physical trauma, coma or stupor. I am confident that we are looking at a purely psychological phenomenon.

We don't want to risk sedating her too heavily, as we were just beginning to get a good cognitive response from her before this episode."

Dr Ward was rubbing her hands together in an uncomfortable manner; Neil felt she had something more on her mind.

"What is it Dr Ward, what are you not telling me?" Neil implored.

"It's not a clinical issue Neil. I am sorry to say this to you but the board of directors have asked for your wife to be transferred out of the clinic. They believe she poses too much of a risk to the clinic staff and the other patients."

Neil couldn't believe what he was hearing.

"You're saying she has to leave here, despite how vulnerable a state she's in. You're joking right?" Neil asked, incredulous.

"I'm sorry Neil, the clinic is set up to protect the patients mainly from themselves." She let out a long sigh, the decision to quit clearly not hers. "We've lost three valued members of our little team, three friends of ours. Your wife's life is obviously in immediate danger, you need to address her security first and her healthcare second. If you can arrange a secure place for her, we can recommend a number of highly qualified private health care professionals who will be able to work exclusively for you." She added, "Perhaps it's time for Natasha to be nursed in the bosom of her loved ones." She grasped Neil's right hand between hers. "I'm so sorry Neil."

## CHAPTER FIFTY EIGHT

**Friends**

Warren made the arrangements. After Brian's recent attempt on her life, Natasha was brought to the ranch. The golf lodge was turned over to nursing and security staff as a makeshift hospital. Local sheriffs posted two men at her bedside 24/7 and regular patrols were made of the grounds and the nearby vicinity. As long as this level of activity persisted, Brian would not get close again.

"Warren, you know this isn't enough! When the hue and cry dies down, Brian will be back, he'll try again!"

"Jesus Neil, give the law a chance, they'll bring him down this time, you'll see. He's in a foreign country, he's alone and he's got a formidable law enforcement agency after his hide. He'll run for sure, and when he does, he'll get caught," Warren reassured.

"No, he won't run. He's like a fucking ghost, he'll stay in the shadows and as soon as we let our guard down he'll pounce again. We have to outwit him Warren, draw him out. We have to outwit him and then kill him. Natasha won't be free while that bastard breathes!"

Perhaps it was a childish gesture, dating back to playground gangs, but Neil felt he needed his army mates around him, needed to draw strength from their good old fashioned male presence. He placed an SOS call to the UK. Jimbo was at home and available. 'Lost Bob' was enjoying a spell of holiday at Her Majesty's pleasure for some stupid misdemeanour so would definitely not be making the trip. Within a few short days, Jimbo had arrived and was bunked down with Goose in one of Warren's numerous dorms which had been built to house film crews if ever the need arose.

"Neil, my CIA contacts have established that Brian's Provo masters have something of an arrangement with an outlaw biker gang in Waco. We can arrange for the Sheriff to have them raided, pick them up and bring them to us. The CIA guys have ways of getting information out of people Neil. We can find out where Brian is holed up," Warren suggested.

"This is our chance Warren. This is something for me and the boys, we speak their language," Neil offered.

"Don't bank on it Neil. Outlaw gangs over here are pretty hardcore," Goose interrupted. "Don't expect any sympathy from these guys. You're well known back home in the UK, the clubs respect you for your work and commitment, but that won't hold any truck here!"

"We speak their language," Neil reiterated. "That has to count for something? I'm not above name dropping; I have some powerful acquaintances on the UK scene who I reckon could smooth the way for us! This is it, this could be our best shot. Does anyone have a better plan?"

Warren looked on, a sceptical expression etched across his brow.

Neil punched his clenched fist into the breakfast bar, causing the nest of knives to bounce out of their sharpening holder. Neil grasped a mean looking butcher's knife from the pile. Holding the knife sharp side up, he pressed the palm of his left hand onto the blade! "Goddamn it Warren, my whole life is balanced on a knife edge, and that fucking lunatic is holding the knife! I promised Natasha that I would protect her, take care of her. So far I've failed at every junction. Dumb luck and her own strength and tenacity are all that have brought her this far; I've been as good as useless!

Warren lifted Neil's hand from the razor sharp surface. A peel of crimson blood dripped from the blade. "Feeling sorry for yourself is pointless self-indulgence Neil. The only thing you're guilty of is underestimating your enemy. That and naturally failing to acknowledge just how evil and determined that somebitch really is!" Warren slammed the point of the weapon into the thick natural wood of the breakfast bar.

"OK Neil, we'll have to see if this plan of yours has legs. It's time we played to our strengths and took the fight to Mr Dix!"

"We need to give the local Harley dealership a call, get ourselves some suitable wheels. Warren, have you got a local phone book I can use?" Neil asked.

"Neil," Warren explained, "the local Harley dealer is a golfing friend; I'll give him a call straight away, see what he's got kicking about, what he can rustle up."

## **CHAPTER FIFTY NINE**

### Candy shop

It took about three days before the first bikes arrived.

Neil rapped on the door of the dorm which Goose and Jimbo were sharing.

"Wakey wakey sleeping beauties! C'mon boys, I want to take a reccy out to these Waco boys' clubhouse, have a look-see at what sort of resources the enemy has at his disposal."

"Is that wise Neil? The last thing we want to do is blow our cover before we're ready to make our move," Goose cautioned.

"I'm not considering calling anyone out Goose, there's nothing to stop us going for a spin on our hogs though, surely?"

"S'pose not, it's a bar isn't it? We can always just order drinks," Goose replied.

"Breakfast first," Jimbo chimed in, "then let's go for a ride!"

Warren was already stood at the hob in the jumbo sized kitchen, a number of pots, pans and 'vittles' spread out noisily on the work surfaces. "Texan breakfasts boys?" Warren asked as the hungry bikers filed in.

"Which consists of?" Jimbo enquired.

"Well, sausage, Texan toast, eggs, hash browns, grits, OJ and coffee, or you can have a little oatmeal and milk, whichever you prefer. Else I can whip yuh up a burger as fat as a town dog. Your call boys?"

"Texan for me Warren," Jimbo replied.

## Bittersweet Humiliation

A round of head nodding confirmed that Texan would be acceptable fare.

Warren got on with the task of organising chow while the boys strolled outside to check out the bikes.

"Wow!" Jimbo exclaimed, looking at the exotic machinery Warren had so far acquired. "This little low-rider has got my name on it! Just call me 'Billy'!" Jimbo had picked out a long low, T barred Panhead, reminiscent of the 'Billy bike' ridden by Dennis Hopper in the iconic film 'Easy Rider'.

Neil plumped for a well ridden UA 74 incher. Unlike Jimbo, Neil hadn't put on weight since his Forces days and was still fitting into his 'original' well-worn leathers. The bike would perfectly suit his look.

Goose of course picked out the most chrome bedecked Shovel Head 1340 he could find to the amusement of the other two.

"What?" Goose exclaimed.

After a moment or two, Jimbo responded with, "You shy retiring bloody wallflower you Goose! Ever the bridesmaid never the bride eh?"

## CHAPTER SIXTY

**Ride out**

After breakfast, as they were suiting up, Jimbo strolled across to Goose and with a fatherly hand on the shoulder said, "You and I have to have a little chat about the letter you sent me when this is all over mate!"

"That was a different moment in a different world mate, forget about it," Goose replied. "All put to bed now!"

"No Goose, this is a different world, but when we go home to the real world when this all blows over, then what?"

"Hey, one crisis at a time eh Jimbo, I promise we'll work on that when this shit is over," Goose solemnly swore.

It was a pleasant morning's ride up to Waco from Marble Falls. If it weren't for the serious nature of the trip, it would have been quite an enjoyable adventure for the three friends.

After a short stop at the start of the cinder road, it was decided that the best approach was just straight up to the roadhouse then to bluff it through as righteous bros on a visit from the UK. The truth being the best lie!

As they pulled onto the roadhouse parking lot, two prospects built like brick shit houses and armed with lethal looking shotguns were dispatched to find out what they wanted.

One of the two made a beeline for Neil. Whistling in through his teeth, he said, "Hombre, chido moto, woo wee!"

Then in an accent thick with a Mexican twang he said, "Crazy bike man, 74 inch WLA?"

"It's a UA 74 inch but I'd say you're close enough!" Neil replied, doing his level best to look disinterested and detached.

"Watcha doin' here boy, you a long way off the beaten track eh? What you want here? You got no business being here." The more hostile of the two was the American Indian who had escorted Brian Dix a few weeks previously. He gestured with the business end of his shotgun and looked to be a shoot first ask questions later kind of guy.

Just as things started to look a little ugly, a full dresser Electra-glide rode onto the lot. Brodie leant the heavy bike over onto its kick-stand and strode over to the newcomers.

"Neil Curland!" he exclaimed, breaking into an enormous smile. "Mr Copper Road Choppers himself."

"Hello!" Neil replied.

Offering Neil a hand to shake he said, "Well I'll be, we've howdied but we haven't shook. The name's Brodie. I'll be damned if I ain't seen all your shows on VCR! Got me an ex Air Force buddy livin' in England sends me all your shows!"

"Pleased to meet you Brodie, you already know my name, my friends are Goose and the big man is Jimbo!"

"Neil, it's a pleasure to have you here man, you and me are kindred spirits; you build some damn fine bikes. A little bird tells me you're bringing the show stateside?" He whistled through his teeth. "Man, you sure are gonna be huge. Maybe got a place for me in your outfit huh?" He took a more serious note. "But you should really whistle before you walk into a stranger's camp, y'know what I'm sayin'? Unannounced visitors are normally as welcome as screwworm." His harsh features broke into a friendly grin. "For the head honcho of Copper Road Choppers though, we'll make an exception. C'mon in boys, grab yourselves a couple of beers and tell me what brings you to Waco?"

They walked into the dimly lit roadhouse interior. The walls were all dark natural wood and the tiny windows afforded little ingress of sunlight.

"Brodie," Neil began, "I'm not going to insult your intelligence by lying to you. We're looking for Brian Dix; we think maybe you can help us find him!"

Brodie's expression went from surprised to contemplative. He gestured for the strangers to join him sitting on bar stools. "Why would I want to do that Neil?"

Neil decided to throw caution to the wind and lay his cards out straight.

"You seem to be a decent bloke Brodie, that's why I'm going to be completely candid with you; my wife has history with Dix. He's a paedophile. He groomed her from the age of fifteen, got her knocked up, then became controlling and abusive."

Neil put his head in his hands and sighed, recalling the events leading up to this moment; the recollections were obviously taking their toll.

"Since then he's systematically destroyed her. He's near enough ended her life, put her through hell on earth. First he kidnapped her child, we managed to get her back, and then he came after my wife." Fearing Brodie may prove to be an adversary Neil was fighting back the tears, preserving the macho image in the face of this unknown character.

"Go on Neil," Brodie prompted. "This shores up the already low opinion I have of our friend Mr Dix."

Neil continued, "He kidnapped her. He managed to get her across to Ireland." He was having obvious trouble keeping the emotion from his wavering voice. "He abused her terribly, got her addicted to a whole host of substances then rented her out to the lowest bidder. She was raped, beaten and abused almost to the point of death." He had Brodie's full attention now and decided to give him the whole story. "He had my unborn child beaten out of her womb, and then made sure she would never be able to conceive again!"

"Jesus H Christ, that boy raised hell and stuck a chunk under it," Brodie said. "The poor bitch, how is she now?"

"She's been through rehab and we've managed to reverse a number of the injuries he inflicted on her. After the most severe beating, after she lost my child, he had her sewn up like a horse so she would survive and he could put her back out to work. She must have been in agony!" Neil paused to give Brodie time to process the information before continuing, "Despite leaving her fighting for her life, despite all he's taken from her, that still wasn't enough; he's come out here, come after her again."

"She's the mark? Jesus! I thought it was someone in witness protection or some gangster," Brodie exclaimed.

"No, I'm afraid it's my wife he's after. Just a plain old 'nut job' after some personal revenge. He tried to take her out in the rehab center last week. Security rumbled him and ran him out, but not until he had taken the life of a cop and three innocent nurses in the process."

"I don't get it," Brodie questioned, "why is he getting support from back home if this is just personal?"

"I've no idea," Neil answered. "Maybe this is a side mission for him or maybe he's fed them a pack of lies. I really have no idea; I've told you pretty much all there is to tell. You know who I am. That's about all I can add."

"D'you have a picture of your wife Neil?" Brodie asked.

"Yes I do," Neil answered, taking a photo taken on their honeymoon from his wallet and passing it to him.

Brodie studied the picture for a while. When the big man passed the photo back, Neil couldn't help but notice the tear in the corner of his eye.

"I wish I could deliver this man's head to you on a platter Neil, I really do!"

"We will do all the dirty work Brodie; we just need your help!"

"I'll help you Neil. Your man is under the protection of an associate club of ours. I can't give him up to you, that would be disloyal to my club and that ain't gonna happen. I can't be seen to help you, as that would be courting trouble from across the pond." Brodie thought for a moment. "The Brady boys are just a bunch of disloyal mules; they'll fight for whoever has the most muscle and cash, but I can't just take your boy back. The way we parted company he would know somethin' was wrong and run for sure."

Brodie kicked open the cooler in the corner of the bar and withdrew another four beers. He handed the drinks out before continuing. "I have no love for Brady MC. In recent years, they've been with us and as often they've been against us. We should wipe them out but they're useful when we've a dirty job to do, y'know what I'm sayin'? Jobs we don't want our prints all over."

"I do," Neil answered.

"Rumour has it we have a rival club, some jokers from down San Antonio way who are looking to expand into our territories, take away some of our 'business interests', you hear me? Chances are they may try to 'patch-over' Brady. So I'm sayin', it don't matter too much to me if Brady get taken down, one way or the other!" Brodie added, "I can give you an address, and I'll tell you what sort of an arsenal they keep, what their weaknesses are. I'll help you any way I can."

They sat for a short while in silence, draining their beers.

"It's time to swap spit and hit the road boys. I wish you luck," Brodie concluded.

As the bikers filed out of the bar, Brodie handed Neil his card. "Neil, if there's anything else I can help you with, give me a call. If it's in my power and it don't compromise me or my club's interests, you got it, understand?"

"I do Brodie, and thank you." As they were mounting their bikes, Brodie called Neil back, he had one more pressing thing on his mind. "Neil, do me a favour, when you see the whites of his eyes, when you can really smell his fear, tell him Tammy says 'hello'."

"I will do Brodie, I will do." Neil had no idea what Brodie was on about, but he knew better than to press him for answers now, after the meeting had gone so well.

# CHAPTER SIXTY ONE

## The plan

Back at the ranch in Marble Falls, Goose burst into the lounge like a man on a mission.

"Eureka!" he exclaimed. "Neil, I've had an idea. Jesus Neil, this is a game changer. I've got us a plan now which could see us in with a powerful chance of putting Brian down once and for all!" Goose beckoned for Neil, Jimbo and Warren to follow him into the study and sit down. Clearly the idea was fairly involved.

"Look, we would need to run this past Brodie," Goose said. "I don't know how much of this is fact and how much is my overactive imagination, but Brodie implied that his club and this other bunch have a bit of an uneasy relationship; they are as often adversaries as allies." Goose paused, allowing the others to catch up.

"Go on," Neil suggested, intrigued.

"Well, I was thinking… Now this may just be me watching too many roadhouse movies in my youth, but I believe the bigger 'outlaw' clubs have a ceremony whereby they will sometimes absorb a smaller club into their ranks, I believe it's known as a patch-over? Brodie did refer to it so I presume it's a fact."

"You have watched too many 'Hells Angles' movies," Jimbo interjected, deliberately getting the name wrong for comedic emphasis.

"Jimbo, you are a knob!" Goose replied.

"Go on Goose, I'm with you. You may have something," Neil encouraged.

"Syphilis, gonorrhoea… A very small willy!" Jimbo suggested.

"Honestly, Jimbo, big as you are, I may be forced to deck you if you don't shut up!" Goose defended.

"Let him talk Jimbo," Neil interrupted. "At the end of the day this is a very serious situation. We need some good suggestions on the table, and I don't think this is as far-fetched as it sounds."

"We run it past Brodie, ask him if there's any situation which would persuade him to patch the Brady MC over to his lot. What I'm thinking is, if we could create a situation whereby Brodie would be obliged to mount a hostile take-over of the rival MC, then perhaps the raiding party could be seeded with a few 'good guys'. I'm thinking that three stout fellows might suffice."

Neil was smiling now, and even the irreverent Jimbo was beginning to sit up and take notice, although that may have just been wind.

Seeing Warren's big face break from a haggard, worried expression to his usual beaming smile brought the first chuckle in a while from the assembled throng.

"He's so clever he can suck his own cock!" Jimbo interjected.

"Oh Mr Jimbo," Goose replied, "I almost forgot you were here, then I smelt your colostomy bag!"

"Surprises me you can smell anything past your fucking breath Goose, you never heard of Tic Tacs?" Jimbo retaliated.

"It's your fucking arse that stinks Jimbo, you're a fucking one man methane factory. It's torture sharing a bunk with you. There's dictators in third world countries committing acts of genocide to control the output of your fucking ring!" Goose shouted back. "No wonder my breath smells, I've been necking your farts all night!"

Jimbo suddenly changed tack and assimilated the accent and mannerisms of a proper English gent. "Since you mention it, I am off for my post breakfast poo; it's been brewing since this morning, so I advise you all to observe a five mile exclusion zone, as there may be fallout!" As he walked towards one of the ranch's numerous luxury bathrooms, Jimbo asked, "Warren, do you have a sink plunger? I usually block the pipes up round at Goose's mum's."

As the man mountain shuffled towards the loo, Neil observed, "I think that round was Jimbo's, Goose!"

"Mmm," Goose replied with a frown. "Does my breath really smell?"

Neil and Warren burst out laughing.

"So come on Goose, now that your distraction has left the room, let's hear the rest of this plan," Neil said.

"I'm thinking that there might just be a little resistance to the take over and that in the ensuing firefight our man might just get hit by a stray bullet. That way, Brodie will come out of it without a stain on his character; just a simple case of a bit of inter-club politics gone awry. Collateral damage as our US partners used to say after they dropped a bit of ordnance on our lines." Goose fell silent, awaiting response to his ideas.

"Lot of loose ends Gee man," Warren interjected. "I still don't see why you don't let the Sheriff's men take care of it, they could mount a raid in half the time it will take you, and with the anger the Sheriff's office are feeling at the moment, you might just find Dix gets caught in the crossfire anyway, legitimately and legally."

"I don't know Warren, we're only going to get one shot and I'm sure that if we miss him he's going to disappear until he surfaces for another go at Natasha. Next time, we may not be so lucky," Neil concluded.

"What say I have a word with the Sheriff, see if they could mount a low key, unconnected raid on the outlaws' clubhouse?" Warren suggested.

"What were you thinking?" Neil replied, obviously confused.

"I am thinking of shelling the enemy, soften them up. Take out the most lethal players before you make your move, maybe avoid a little bloodshed."

"I think I'll try running the scenarios past Brodie. I don't know why, but I just feel that he's a man we can trust."

"I hope you're right Neil; it'll be too late when you find you've got a rattler by the tail!" Warren added soberly.

Neil called Brodie up and outlined to him both ideas they'd been discussing.

"Forget the Sheriff's men straight off Neil. Zack Gantz has numerous contacts in the County Sheriff's department. I don't want to know how you discovered our involvement with the Irishman, but I can tell you this: if the Sheriff's department had known, we would've too! Your patch-over idea ain't so stupid though, maybe somethin' we can do there. You won't be able to tag along with my boys though, it don't work that way. This goes down, it goes down between clubs; outsiders would raise questions. If the Irishman's there, we'll have to take him back. Maybe I can win back his trust, let him know that we've brought him in 'cause he's in danger from the club rivalry, then find a way to set him up, deliver him to you." Brodie paused for a second, took a breath, then said, "Where you at? I'm thinkin' I might take a ride over, in the morning, see if we can't get our heads together on this!"

"Hold on a second Brodie," Neil said. Holding his hand over the mouthpiece, he asked the others if it was OK for Brodie to visit.

Warren glanced at Goose and Jimbo for their approval before nodding his assent.

"Yeah, that sounds like a good plan," Neil answered before giving the address and directions to him.

"Put some grits and a pot of coffee on the stove, I'll be round about breakfast time!" Brodie confirmed.

"The place is surrounded by lawmen Brodie, but don't worry, we'll brief them that you're not the enemy, so they won't give you any hassle."

"I'll ditch the cut then Neil, just so as not to arouse suspicion."

"Can you do that?" Neil asked, naively.

"Puhlease Neil," Brodie replied. "It's been a long time since I was a prospect, I do what the fuck I like!"

"We'll look forward to seeing you tomorrow Brodie," Neil answered, slightly embarrassed.

"Best we put a ring of steel round the little lady before he gets here, just in case this is all a plot to try and hurt her again," Warren warned.

## CHAPTER SIXTY TWO

**Hero**

The sun had not long been up when the burble of Brodie's Glide pulled up outside the gated entrance. The cops and the hired guards questioned him quickly, then opened the gates and waved him through.

Neil and Warren stood on the veranda, overlooking the parking area. The ranch did not sport a conventional front door, a testament to Nell's love of family and being outdoors. Visitors joined in whatever was taking place on the vast raised family area before retiring further into the sprawling, opulent but at the same time homely residence.

Brodie came to a dignified stop on the gravel before leaning the huge Harley onto its kick-stand and dismounting.

"Howdy Mr Brodie," Warren exclaimed, extending a massive hand to shake the equally large digits of Brodie.

"Well ain't that just sweeter than a baby's breath!" Brodie exclaimed, somewhat humbled. "Warren Bateson, as I live and breathe. You're only my goddamn childhood hero. That biker movie you made with Burt and Jack was the inspiration for my life! How the hell are you man?" he exclaimed, cupping his hand around Warren's in a genuine gesture of admiration and respect.

"Tell truth, right now I feel lower than a gopher hole," Warren replied. "But I'm mighty hoping that you might be able to help us change that Mr Brodie!"

"Hell, it's just Brodie, I ain't got the time for no misters."

"Well in that case, I'm Warren, and I'm real pleased to make your acquaintance Brodie!"

Coffee was taken *al fresco* as Goose and Jimbo roused from their slumber and joined the group on the veranda.

Neil sat down and began the conversation, outlining the plan they had discussed the previous night.

"Yeah cool Neil, but first things first," Brodie interrupted. "I want to meet your wife, is she here? I want to meet Natasha!" Neil looked a little shocked, concerned. The group fell into an uneasy silence.

"Hey man, you can search me, handcuff me if you like. You have nothing to fear from me, but if you want my help, I want to meet the lady at the center of all this; see her with my own eyes," Brodie declared.

"OK Brodie," Neil said. "We'll have some breakfast and Warren can call through to the lodge, tell them we're coming then we'll go on over, and you can meet Natasha.

Two golf carts transported them across the short distance to the lodge where the substantial security detail checked them all thoroughly; they had been briefed to keep up the vigilance no matter who or what.

Inside, Neil spoke briefly to the nurse whom he was on familiar terms with, since he spent all of his free time there.

"How is she Della?" he enquired.

"No change I'm afraid Neil," the nurse replied. "She is off sedation now but she's still completely unresponsive. If we put food or drink into her mouth, she swallows. If we take her to the bathroom regularly she will respond, but apart from that she's a ghost. Doctor's coming to see her shortly."

Brodie followed, flanked by Jimbo who looked tense like a coiled snake, ready to pounce on his worthy adversary should the need arise.

The group walked into the room. Natasha lay on her side in the small hospital bed. Wires snaked out from parts of her body, connected to machines which whirred and beeped constantly.

Thanks to the work of the most eminent doctors the country had to offer, superficially, Natasha had made a remarkable recovery. Externally, it was hard to tell the torment she had endured. The damage, significant damage, was concealed below the surface.

Despite her surroundings, Natasha wore her own nightie, her long curly hair had been meticulously brushed, her make-up applied faithfully and to her own design as well as Neil and photographs could describe it. This was all part of the gentle rehabilitation programme she was following. Shortly, she would be raised from the bed, dressed in her own clothes and sat near to the window, where she would be able to watch her children playing, supervised in the paddock. It was all in the desperate hope that something would trigger her return and bring her back to the land of consciousness and cognitive control.

Brodie pulled the sheet back slightly, exposing Natasha's face, her hair and the nape of her neck.

"She's beautiful Neil," he exclaimed, a tear welling in the corner of his eye. "So very beautiful!" he reinforced, the tears now blatantly flowing down his cheeks.

Confused, Neil replied, "I know Brodie, she's been through so much, so much pain and torture. I can't begin to describe to you the things that Brian Dix has done to her, what he's put her through."

"I've seen that vacant stare before, on the face of the last girl that bastard hurt," Brodie whispered. "I'll help you Neil. If the Irishman is at the Brady clubhouse, we'll get to him, and we'll kill him!"

Returning to the main ranch, a fresh round of coffees was rustled up. The plan was discussed. Goose recalled something Brodie had mentioned previously about a rival MC making inroads into his club's territory.

"What about if this rival MC's soldiers were seen in sufficient numbers around the Brady lot's territory, would that give you a credible excuse to attack them?" Goose enquired.

"Well, that would for sure give us reason enough to sit at the table and vote. I think I can persuade my boys to vote my way," Brodie concluded.

"Good, then it's on to the next stage," Goose said smugly.

"What are you thinking Goose?" Neil asked.

"Can you get us the skinny on this rival club from down San Antonia way Brodie? We need to get a photograph of their cut-off design, so we can copy their patches down to the last embroidered dot."

"I'm sure that won't be a problem. I need to make a call to my guy in Ireland, tell him that Dix's security is compromised and we need to snatch him back," he replied. "That should get us credibility from over the water and stop this storm landing back on me."

Goose turned to Warren. "Can you get your wardrobe people to make us some costumes Warren? We need cut-off jackets, complete with full patch colours. We need some authentic border accents too if we're going to fool anyone. There are a good number of our boys who settled over here and a few ex US military from Germany who still wear the 'Booze Brothers' badge." Goose paced around the room a couple of times, stroking his beard, deep in thought. "It'll take a day or two but I reckon we could round up at least another three or four bodies at short notice."

"Guys," Warren interrupted, "what you need are some convincing actors to play the lead roles. Let me make some phone calls, I reckon I can rustle up a few hell raising aspiring actors who would jump at this chance, especially with the promise of a studio contract at the end of the performance!"

"Discretion is our utmost priority Warren, one weak link takes us all down," Goose warned. "What would the fallout be like if things got bloody Warren?"

"Any casualties from the other side wouldn't pose a problem Gee, they're outlaws, we're still pretty nineteenth century when it comes to outlaw bikers in Texas, but if any of you Brits are taken down, for that matter any of the good guys, that would for sure be a big hole in the fence!"

"Then we are going to have to make sure we field the right boys at the front and keep the extras out of the scene! Good eh Warren? Got the vernacular see," Goose joked. "Now what time do we have over in the UK?" he thought out loud, pondering his watch. "Can I borrow your phone Warren?"

"Sure Gee man, help yourself," Warren replied.

"We need to get our fake outlaws together here and get 'em on bikes!" Neil announced.

Warren interjected, "I can handle that Neil, we can't get many more bikes from the local guys but if I get my procurement people on it, they have the sort of connections to get this sorted quickly! All Harleys I take it?"

"That'll be just the ticket Warren, no showroom stuff though. Chops, hogs and rats. We want to look like saddle tramps. That should get us through casual scrutiny."

"Well I guess you boys have enough to be getting on with. I'll take my leave. Let me know when you're good to go so I can knock doors and ring bells my end." Brodie grabbed Neil's hand in a high thumb grip, thumped his back and said, "Stay strong buddy, don't fuck up now, Brady are mean mother fuckers. You get caught with your pecker out, you gonna wish you'd left things alone."

"I'm afraid that's not an option Brodie!"

"I hear you bro!" Brodie offered his hand to Warren in a more traditional handshake. "Hey, I'm real proud to have met you man. You keep it together and tell Jack and Burt from me that they're real fucking gods, you hear?"

Warren caught hold of Brodie's hand, twisted his palm round to encircle Brodie's thumb, the way he had seen his biker brethren do countless times. "Hey Brodie, it's me that's proud to have met you. If we pull this off, I'll see to it that you get to meet your heroes, and I'll make sure they know that you're their equal." He spoke with real sincerity.

"Be seeing you all soon." Brodie strolled across to his Harley, effortlessly kicked the motor into life and manhandled the big bike back out of the drive and away.

Goose made a number of calls. One of the recipients was 'Mad Bob', one of the members of the 'Booze Brothers' who was well connected in wider circles. After a lengthy conversation, followed by him making a number of other calls, he returned, triumphant.

Warren took Goose's return as his cue to adjourn to the office where he could make the calls necessary to set the wheels in motion for his part of the plan. "I'll make a few calls, get the relevant people started on making this little masquerade happen guys." With that, he left the breakfast table and the room.

"Did you manage to contact those ex US military boys, are they up for a skirmish?"

"Come up trumps there," Goose enthused, grinning from ear to ear. "Got a couple of loyal 'Booze Brothers' motoring up from Tucson. Bloody perfect, they're practically Mexicans. Got their own hogs too so that's another plus." Goose punched a fist into the air.

"Goose, I will never doubt you again!" Neil replied soberly.

It took some time to get all the props and players together.

Brodie proved a highly resourceful ally. He provided them with a disused grain barn where they could assemble the bikes and tutor their motley crew of warriors outside the glare of publicity and police activity that surrounded Warren's ranch.

Contrary to the maverick way the law enforcement agencies are portrayed in Hollywood movies, in reality, they tend to do as they're told: follow protocol and the chain of command. Right now Warren's VIP connections, which extended right from the Mayor up to Capitol Hill, were pressuring them to allow the comings and goings on the ranch to proceed unimpeded and without question. So far, they were obliging.

With Goose and Jimbo handling the task of briefing the players on their individual roles and Warren's people organising the bikes and props, Warren was able to catch up with his demanding work schedule. Neil was free to spend time with his children and to visit Natasha.

## CHAPTER SIXTY THREE

**Shell shocked**

"I don't get it Doc," Neil began. "She's back here with her family, she's safe and loved, why can't we reach her?"

Doctor Regina Ward, the psychiatrist from the clinic, had arranged a sabbatical to continue treating Natasha exclusively.

"Neil, I can't begin to imagine the horrors she's experienced. Just the cocktail of drugs she's been exposed to would have been enough to see lesser spirits broken. We've witnessed people with symptoms like hers who've been in situations of extreme stress, war zones and the like, often where they were completely powerless to help themselves. We call it trauma beyond the range of normal human experience, or post-traumatic stress disorder. Natasha's case is one of the worst I have ever witnessed; she is pretty much catatonic. We were only just starting to make meaningful progress with her when this latest episode pushed her over the edge again." She placed a concerned hand on the back of Neil's arm as he gently stroked a stray hair from Natasha's eye. She stared out into space, the pupils of her eyes merely pin pricks. Her normally crystal clear eyes appeared foggy, somehow cloudy.

"Will she come back Doc?" Neil asked.

"Talk to her Neil; direct your questions at her. She can hear you for sure. We don't know how this mental psychosis works, how the mind cuts itself off from the brain like this, but we do know for sure that her ears and eyes are still working, still processing all the information that's going in." She looked a little awkward, as if she wasn't sure about something. Neil picked up on it immediately.

"What is it Doctor? Doctor Ward, c'mon, after all the shit that's gone down I need total disclosure. If there's something I need to know then please, spit it out."

She hesitated. "Neil, come with me into another room. I don't want to discuss this in front of your wife."

They walked along the hallway into one of the stockrooms still filled with golfing paraphernalia.

"Neil, you know that Natasha's physician advised that she had sustained a fractured skull at some point during her incarceration?"

"Yes, I was aware of that," Neil replied.

"Well, it's not really my field, but some of the symptoms exhibited by your wife could be indicative of damage sustained to the frontal cortices of the brain. When the skull is accelerated quickly due to a blow to the head…"

"I know how it works Doc, I've been there myself," Neil interrupted. "The underside of the brain scrapes against the back of the eye sockets and the bridge of the nose. A little damage goes a long way!"

"I don't believe that's the case with Natasha. I genuinely believe this to be a mental disorder rather than a physical one. From her case notes, it's suggested that she was cognitive before she overdosed and during her detox withdrawal she exhibited typical responses," Doctor Ward said. "I sincerely believe the best course of action for Natasha is to convince her that she is safe and sound; safe to come back to reality. I would like you to make her life as normal as possible. She shows a typical catatonic response which we call 'waxy flexibility'. Basically, we can put her in any position and she will stay there, so she can sit up OK in a wheelchair. Take her and the children for short walks in the grounds, sit and watch TV together. Physically, she is out of the woods. Now it's all about her mental health."

"I'm afraid that's out of the question Doc," Neil confided. "Natasha's physical well-being is still very much at risk from outside forces. Until we can lay that spectre to rest, I'm afraid she will have to remain here, a virtual prisoner. I'll spend as much time with her as I possibly can. I'll bring the kids in to see her, it's high time they did. Maybe that will spark some reaction from her."

"If you think the kids would be OK with that. I think that would be a very good idea," she agreed.

"It's time. The kids know that Mum's here, they know she's ill, but they, especially Monica, can't understand why they can't see her. Natasha looks herself again now; I think it's time the kids were reunited with her, for all their sakes."

"OK Neil, let me know when you want to bring them over and I'll make sure that Mummy is looking her best."

Neil suddenly paled, his stoic reserve collapsed completely and he dissolved into a mess of tears.

"Oh God, Neil, I'm so sorry," Doctor Ward consoled. "I'm so sorry, what did I say?"

Neil composed himself, raising the emotional barriers back up after their momentary breach. "It's not your fault Doctor Ward, it was just, you calling Natasha 'mummy', it holds so many mixed emotions."

"I understand Neil. Natasha is not the only one affected by this tragedy. Sometimes we overlook the walking wounded."

"No Doc, I'm not looking for sympathy. Natasha has been through hell and back; my problems are nothing compared to hers. I'm not about to break down and get needy when I have to be strong for her. She deserves that at least after what I've let that bastard do to her," he expressed solemnly.

"Blaming yourself for this is a dangerous route to go down Neil. This whole sequence of sorry events was orchestrated in the disturbed mind of a psychopath. Everything you've done has been reactionary. Nothing that has happened is as a result of your actions. You're a victim, just as much as Natasha."

"I've neither the time nor the inclination to play the victim Doc!" With renewed resolve, Neil left the conversation hanging and walked out of the lodge, back towards the main ranch.

## CHAPTER SIXTY FOUR

**Deception**

All the players were assembled, dressed in their impressive counterfeit 'cuts' emblazoned with the patches of the rival club. It was time to begin the first act in the masquerade. With a final pep talk from Neil, the impressive collection of a dozen bikes fired into life before riding out from the barn double file onto the dirt road.

Like a squadron of Spitfires and Hurricanes they howled onto the highway and roared towards the town of Brady.

At the front rode the two American natives – the bikers from Tucson. Gnarled and sun browned, riding scruffy road-worn hogs, they were the ones who would pass more intensive scrutiny. Following close behind were a couple of the hired 'extras' courtesy of Warren. They were Californians and too much down time on the beach had given them the desired look; it was an easy task to turn beach bums into saddle tramps.

Neil had ditched the side valve 1200 on Brodie's advice and settled for the reliability and inconspicuousness of an Ironhead Sportster instead. Along with the other Brits he was bringing up the rear, not convinced that their theatre make-up would pass much more than a cursory inspection, especially in the afternoon heat. Neil, Jimbo and Goose had elected to wear just the cloned bottom rockers on their 'cuts', surmising that as prospects they would be unlikely to be approached.

## Bittersweet Humiliation

As the convoy rode into town they attracted a fair bit of attention. Like a scene out of an old Spaghetti Western, mothers ran into the road, gathered their prize ewe lambs to their bosoms and scuttled back to the security of their homes, convinced that they were witnessing the beginning of the apocalypse.

The first mission was to be noticed. Mission accomplished.

Following the game plan, they pulled up at the local bar and pool hall. First through the door were the two ex US soldiers. They had joined the 'Booze Brothers' years before when stationed at Herogen Camp in Western Germany. Belonging to the US Combat Equipment Battalion, they were kind of on a par with the Royal Air Force regiment 'Rock Apes'. They were big blokes, just like the 'Apes' – strong and volatile but bereft of much subtlety. They made straight for the pool table without taking much notice of any local etiquette with regards to waiting your turn.

The local rednecks were incensed and within a few moments they were sitting on a powder keg. Only a tiny spark was required. It came when one of the bikers lent over to take a shot and exposed his $14^{th}$ CEC insignia tattooed on his arm.

"What the fuck you wearing there boy? You gotta goddamn US Army badge there and you wearin' sissy boy biker colours over the top?" the lead redneck yelled, pulling the biker's shirt sleeve up. "CEC, you fucking yeller bellied kit monkey. Why didn't you join the real army boy? You just let us do the fightin' for you huh?"

The redneck pulled his shirt up, exposing the Marine Corps tattoo emblazoned there. "That's the Corps badge you fucking retards, you kiss my ass before you swan in here taking over our goddamn pool hall."

The biker pulled his shirt down over his ink. "You have a problem with us Jarhead?"

"Yea' I have a problem with you pussies swanning in here and helping yourselves to our pool tables!" the redneck replied.

"Tell you what," the biker answered, "you want a table? Why don't you run down the Quartermaster stores, ask about you getting a table. He'll fix you right up."

"Filling out a requisition, in triplicate, won't take but an hour or so," the other biker added. "Oh hell, I forgot, you Jarheads can't read or write. Tell you what, you just go draw him a pretty picture, he'll sort you right out!"

That was it. Light the red touch paper and stand back.

Pandemonium broke out! It was like a scene from a Clint Eastwood film; fists, bottles and pool cues were bouncing off heads and bodies. By the time the fight was over everyone in Brady knew that there were new kids on the block.

As the bikers departed the bar, victorious, one of the US army guys turned to the other and said, "Don't matter where you's at, you can always trust a Jarhead to kick off. God bless 'em!"

"Yeah, I hope we didn't hurt 'em too much, I gotta lot o' love and respect for Marines!"

"Ahh, they'll be fine. Jarheads thrive on a good punch up, most excitement they've seen in years!"

With that, the boys did a few burnouts and wheelies along the main street, just to emphasise how bad they were!

## Bittersweet Humiliation

Rumour was rife. To ride into town with such audacity these interlopers must have been in league with Brady MC or they must have been there to patch over the local club. The scene was set. Now it was Brodie's move!

## CHAPTER SIXTY FIVE

**Reunion**

Back at Warren's ranch the bikers were in high spirits. Their mission had, in all probability, been a total success. The UK 'Booze Brothers' contingent had not had contact with the stateside members in a good number of years, so partying was the order of the day as was a foregone conclusion of such a reunion – serious drinking.

Warren and his wife, Nell, albeit with the help of one of Warren's location catering companies, laid on a proper Texan cookout complete with a local live band. The group were awesome and they could play both types of music; country *and* western. Proper biker 'shit kickin' stuff. The mood was raucous! With the man hugs and congratulatory shoulder thumps dispensed with, Neil was acutely feeling that the most important part of the jigsaw was missing. He slipped away from the gregarious crowd and made his way to the golf lodge.

Reassuringly he was stopped twice by armed security on his way along the half mile or so of shale road which led to the golf lodge. The entrance to the lodge was locked and the doorway guarded by a further two armed security men. As Neil approached, five thousand watts of security lights burst into life, illuminating the approach to the lodge from all sides. Recognising Neil immediately they requested that he lift his upper garments and turn around slowly, just to check that he was there of his own free will and not rigged with explosives or any other threats. It was a procedure that had been suggested by the security firm and the Sheriff's office. Neil was more more than happy to comply. If it kept Natasha safe it was no inconvenience.

"Evening Mr Curland," the chief guard said. "How's the party going?"

"Everyone's in high spirits," Neil replied. "I didn't want to be a party pooper, but I just couldn't be there, not with Natasha stuck in here like a prisoner."

"We won't let any harm come to her Mr C, you can be sure of that," he reassured Neil.

"That's a comfort to hear guys."

Neil softly knocked on the door of the suite which had become Natasha's dorm, her cell.

The spyglass in the door briefly flashed as the nurse inside inspected the visitor. Nothing was left to chance.

"Hi Della," Neil greeted. "You draw the short straw again?"

"I love the graveyard shift Neil," the nurse replied. "It gives me a chance to catch up on my studying. Besides, I love to watch her sleep; she looks so peaceful and calm."

"She's so beautiful," Neil remarked. "She looks her old self when she's sleeping. She looks so haunted when she's awake." He added, "If you can call it awake."

"She is beautiful Neil. I hope when this is all over and she's fully recovered I can get to know her. I spend so much time sitting talking to her that she must know me as well as she knows herself."

"Do you think she can hear you?" Neil asked.

"I think she does hear things. She doesn't show any significant response, but when I talk about you sometimes I feel her breathing rhythm changes, speeds up, as though she's anxious, trying to show me that she hears."

"Can I have a few moments alone with her please Della?" Neil asked.

"Of course you can Neil. I'll go and sit in the rest room. Lock the door behind me. Just knock on the radiator when you want me back." It was a little routine they'd worked out as there was no intercom between the rooms.

"Thanks Della," he replied.

Natasha's breathing was deep and regular. Neil had the feeling that she wasn't dreaming.

"Natasha," he softly whispered, close to her ear. "I hope you can hear me. Darling Natasha, I need you to come back to me. I love you so much; I can't bear life without you." He stroked a stray lock of hair from her cheek, coaxed the wayward curl back behind her ear. Tears were streaming down his cheeks. "I miss you my love, please, please Natasha, come back, I need to hear your voice again, the children need you so much. They don't understand how Mummy can be here but not hugging them, holding them." He gently brushed his lips against her cheek. "Little David fell over yesterday; he grazed his knee quite badly. He wanted his mummy. It broke my heart to hear him crying out for you. I try so hard Natasha, but I can't be you. You're so warm, so gentle; you make the children feel safe and secure. They need you honey. I need you. Can't you please find your way back home to us?" Natasha's breathing did speed up a little, and her lips parted slightly as she took a deep breath. Neil's hopes soared for a second, but her breathing soon settled back into the previous regular pattern.

"We're here for you baby, we'll always be here. I promise you I'll protect you, I'll keep you safe, even if it costs me my own life!" Neil reassured her with sincerity.

Again, Natasha's breathing increased momentarily before settling back into a regular rhythm.

He sat for nearly an hour, talking, whispering, crying and laughing, telling Natasha all his news. He shared with her the minor details of his and the children's lives; all the little things which only a mother and father would concern themselves with. This had become the routine of Neil's life since Natasha had been moved to the lodge.

He was determined that she would still share in the children's lives, even if she could not respond. Tomorrow, he would bring the children in to see her. They could hold her hand and kiss her; perhaps their closeness would bring her back.

Neil rapped on the radiator. Moments later Della knocked softly at the door. Neil checked the spyglass then opened the door.

"How is she? Any change?" Della asked.

"No," Neil replied. "Her breathing does change, but I am not sure it's in response to anything I may have said. I think it's probably just patterns. I don't know. What do you think?"

"I sit with her for hours Neil, and I honestly think that she hears everything you say when she's asleep. When she's awake, she's deep, deep down, catatonic; her eyes are open but there's no gateway to her mind. When she's asleep, it's like she's closer to the surface." She shrugged. "It makes no sense, I know, but I just believe that's the case."

"I hope so Della, God, I really hope so. I don't want her to lose all this time. Her time with the children is so precious, they mean so much to her!"

# CHAPTER SIXTY SIX

**Surplus**

In the roadhouse the rumours had come flooding in. At the Waco clubhouse tempers were running hot. The bikers in Brady were courting a patch club from out of town, it was a flagrant challenge. Brodie won his vote; his club decided to ride straight over to Brady to patch them over, or to put them out of business, permanently.

The phone in the workshop, Brodie's private phone, rang.

"Brodie," he announced to the caller.

"Mr Brodie, it's Doherty here," the static voice from another continent said. "Brodie, we've had a slight change of plans. Are you listening?"

"I hear you Mr Doherty," Brodie replied.

"Our Mr Dix it seems has stirred up a bit of a hornet's nest, so he has. Long story short and all that Mr Brodie, we would prefer it if Mr Dix did not return home!"

"What about his assignment?" Brodie questioned, trying to get as much information as possible from the exchange.

"There is no assignment Mr Brodie, that's all you need to know. Mr Dix is surplus to requirements. I'm sure you'll have no conscience over dispatching him on our behalf, should the opportunity arise." There was a slight pause before he followed up with, "Next month's collection, if you're successful, you keep it, share it out as you see fit, call it a small gesture of our gratitude. Goodbye Mr Brodie."

With that the receiver went dead.

# **CHAPTER SIXTY SEVEN**

**Rivals**

The Waco bikers outnumbered the Brady club by two to one. Brady MC were completely unprepared. Sat at the conference table discussing the recent appearance of uninvited bikers in their town, they had only posted two prospects as sentries to guard the roadhouse entrance. With their senses dulled from too much indulgence in their own product, they were easily overpowered without a shot being fired.

Brodie kicked in the door to the conference room and delivered his rehearsed speech about the Brady bikers cosying up to some out of town MC and that the time had come to patch over.

"What the fuck Brodie?" Zack Gantz questioned.

Brodie grabbed him by the shoulder and led him out into the hallway. A couple of Waco prospects followed them out, but Brodie shooed them back into the conference room.

"You knew this day was coming Zack," Brodie snarled.

"What the fuck Brodie? What the hell is this?" Gantz reiterated.

"The Irishman Zack, where is he?" Brodie questioned.

"This is about that fucked up psycho? Fuck Brodie, why didn't you just call? I would've told you, that mother fucker lit out of here a week ago after screwing up the hit and losin' me two of my prospects." He shrugged Brodie's hand off his shoulder. "Fuck Brodie, all this for a mother fucker that ain't worth shit?"

"You had this comin' from way back Zack. The Irishman? That's just business." He led Gantz back towards the conference room. "Put on your party smile Zack, we got us a ceremony to perform!"

## CHAPTER SIXTY EIGHT

**Marked man**

Warren walked into the lounge. "Neil, phone call, it's Brodie."

This was the call Neil had waited for. He hoped it would be to inform him that in the clash between rival gangs Brian Dix had been caught in the crossfire and killed. He returned from the call ashen faced.

"Well?" Goose demanded.

"The raid went off as planned. Brodie thanked us all for the cracking job we did as the rival bike club." Neil was still looking down at his feet.

"But?" Goose questioned, impatiently.

"Brian wasn't there," Neil answered, clearly crestfallen. "Damn, damn, damn! Now what?" Warren asked.

"Brodie says that Brian's handlers have put a bounty on his head, that Brian has turned 'loose cannon' and they want him taken down."

"What the hell does that mean?" Jimbo asked. "I can't make head nor tail of it."

"Brodie thinks it means that Brian was working his own agenda with Natasha, that maybe she wasn't the mark and he was moonlighting when he should have been doing a job for his bosses." Neil took a deep breath. "One thing's for sure; Brian's burned all his bridges now, he's run out of friends. It has to be just a matter of time before someone catches up to him!"

"Amen to that," Warren added.

## **CHAPTER SIXTY NINE**

**Surveillance**

Brian thanked good fortune that his instincts had told him to bug Brodie's phone. The man was instinctively cautious and his exchanges over the wires were clipped and non-specific. But nevertheless a few eavesdropped conversations had given Brian intelligence he was not expecting. At first, he had only listened into Brodie's calls sporadically, scanning for calls between Ireland and the US, hoping to glean some snippets of information with which he could gauge his standing back home. A chance interception of the recent exchange between Brodie and Neil Curland had changed that. Initially it was quite a shock, discovering the connection between Brodie and his nemesis, especially hearing them discussing his impending culling. Now he was monitoring Brodie's calls regularly for clues as to Natasha's whereabouts and any possible vulnerability. He would finish this mission with or without sanction from home. Now it was a fight for survival.

Brodie was struggling with a particularly stubborn engine mount. The phone's insistent peal caused him to curse as he reached for a corner of clean rag to wipe the grease from his hands. "Brodie," he barked into the phone impatiently.

"Hi honey," the soft voice purred at the other end of the line.

"Tarina!" he exclaimed in a hoarse whisper, surprised. Cupping his hand around the mouthpiece, he said, "Hi baby, what's up? You know you shouldn't phone me here."

Tarina was a beautiful young Hispanic girl in her late twenties. Brodie had been her saviour, in the right place at the right time to rescue her from an abusive relationship some years before. He had been just a rank and file member of the club then, so he couldn't bring her to the clubhouse as she would have had to serve her apprenticeship and he was not about to share this treasure.

It was a difficult task, but he set her up in a flat, paid for her to finish high school and graduate Nursing College. Tarina was now fully qualified and working in one of the hospitals in Waco. Brodie was understandably proud of his secret love, but he remained keen to keep her and his club life distinctly separate. Since taking over as club president the task had become easier. Of course, the club knew about her, but it was Brodie's business and that was that.

Tarina's love for Brodie was unconditional. If her role was to be his mistress and the club his wife then so be it; he was worth it.

"Honey, I'm sorry. My car's broken down. I was kinda hoping you might come get me? I'm a bit stranded. Sorry honey."

"Aw no, don't be sorry babe, course I'll come rescue you. Where are you?" Brodie consoled.

"I'm just outside of work; staff parking lot opposite ER."

"Go back into work, wait for me there. I'll get the truck and come get you."

Brian put the Citizens Band radio down. Intercepting this call had given him insight into the man, insight into his weakness; women. Unlike himself Brodie was a romantic, a man with a love and respect for women and despite all the macho bluff and bluster he was in love, as it transpired, with a civilian; a woman outside of the biker scene, outside their protection. This knowledge was gold; Brodie had an Achilles heel which could be exploited.

It took Brodie about a half an hour to finish up and fetch the breakdown truck. As he motored off towards the hospital he failed to notice the blue Camaro drop in behind him, two cars back.

## CHAPTER SEVENTY

**To trap a rat**

"We stay on high alert until we confirm Brian's demise," Neil stated.

"That boy's more slippery than a pocketful of pudding. I won't believe he's gone until I have him pegged out as buzzard bait!" Warren confessed.

"Dammit Warren," Neil cursed. "How is it that the bastard is always one step ahead of us?"

"He's feral Neil, probably lived on his wits since he was a kid. Add his mental disposition into the mix and you have a pure recipe for survival. No matter how hard we concentrate, we still can't help interacting with friends, getting on with those around us, fretting and worrying about the problems of others." Warren was still talking as he opened the fridge and opened a cold one for the two of them. He handed a beer to Neil. "That sadistic animal has none of our trappings. He lives for himself, in the moment; no remorse, no guilt, and no distractions. I wouldn't glamorise him as a killing machine, but if he puts his mind to it he certainly gives it one hundred percent."

"So how do we beat him?" Neil questioned.

"Well, if this was one of my film scripts I'd be looking to the writers to work out some sort of a trap; a trap baited with a meal that a wild dog wouldn't be able to resist."

"With me as the bait you mean?"

"Not with you as bait Neil, with Natasha!" Warren delivered the last line in a barely audible whisper.

"I can't believe you would even suggest that Warren. There's not a hope in hell that I would consider putting her in harm's way after what she's been through."

"Now don't go getting your panties in a wad Neil, I ain't suggesting we expose the gal to danger, but there's no stopping us from pretending we have."

"I don't follow you."

"No, for sure you don't. I'm talking we transfer the whole kit and caboodle to someplace else. Make like Natasha's had a turn and has been transferred to another clinic somewhere. We clear out the lodge, bring the real Natasha over to the house with just the essential nursing staff. We put the place on lockdown; a few key security staff. Nobody comes in and nobody leaves until Brian is caught or killed. In the meantime, you and the boys hang out near to the clinic close to the decoy to make Brian think she's there and you're looking out for her. If he's still here, it should smoke him out!"

"I can't leave Natasha here and not be around to protect her!" Neil observed.

Warren laid a thick hand on Neil's shoulder. "That's exactly what I'm hoping Brian's gonna think, and that's exactly why you're gonna have to!"

# CHAPTER SEVENTY ONE

**Reinforcements**

Brodie parked his Harley up in the private lot outside the nursing home. From the number of hired security staff surrounding the place, he could be forgiven for thinking the President of the USA was receiving treatment there.

"Great to see you again Brodie!" Neil said with genuine affection.

"Likewise Neil, how's our little broken angel doing?"

"No real change I'm afraid. All the physical scars have healed but we still can't reach her."

"Give it time Neil; these things operate to their own timetable. She'll come back when she's ready to."

"I hope you're right Brodie, I sincerely hope you're right."

"She here?" Brodie questioned.

Neil glanced around furtively before directing Brodie to the sumptuous leather chairs in the reception waiting area.

"She's back at Warren's. We moved her back into the main house with skeleton staff and low key security. That's why we've turned this place into Fort Knox. It's a decoy to try to lure the bastard out into the open.

"Try to trap a rat?" Brodie glanced around. "He's a slippery goddamn son of a bitch Neil, make no mistake."

"We're staying away from the ranch house right now in case he's scoping us. If he follows any one of us, it'll bring him right back here," Neil said. "Goose and Jimbo are camped out with me in the Romero Hotel. We take it in shifts to ride over here and then hang around so if he's casing this place or the hotel he should get our scent."

"I think I might go on home and pick up a few provisions, come on back and hole up in the hospice. I'd sure like to rekindle my acquaintance with Mr Dix."

"You're more than welcome Brodie." As an afterthought, Neil said, "Probably best to leave the Harley behind though. Can't hurt to keep Brian in the dark about your involvement."

"You're right, best I make a move before he makes me," Brodie added.

## CHAPTER SEVENTY TWO

**Ambush**

The day was just beginning to cool into dusk as he slowed the Electra Glide to negotiate an alley narrowed by parked cars and dumpsters.

He barely caught a glimpse of the Camaro in the half light as it sucker punched into the side of his bike, smashing his leg and pinning him between the bike, the kerb, and the car's fender.

"You son of a bitch!" he cursed between waves of intense pain. "I am going to make you sorry you ever drew breath boy!"

Brian let him thrash about for a few moments, making sure he was well and truly immobilised before stepping out of the car and examining his predicament. "No... No, I don't really think you'll be doing that at all now will you?" Brian laughed sarcastically, lapsing back into his Irish accent as he always did when things were going his way.

Brodie was vulnerable; his trapped legs useless. He was holding the front fender of the car with both hands to keep his pinned torso off the glowing exhaust.

"Perfect!" Brian exclaimed as he proceeded to wind Brodie's wrists up with black gaffer tape.

Once he had Brodie's wrists bound and strapped to his waist he reversed the car back slightly. Temporarily attached to the car from the impact the bike shifted before resting over on its side and breaking loose. Brodie was lying in the road, clear of the bike but in no fit state to move on his own. Both his legs were crushed.

Brian grabbed him by the belt. It was immediately evident that he would have very little chance of manhandling the uncooperative man-mountain into the small car alone.

Relieved of having to hold his body weight away from the exhausts Brodie clung to the frame of the smashed Electra Glide. His upper body strength was proving more than the comparatively scrawny Brian could negotiate.

"Bitten off more than you can chew again, huh Irish?" Brodie spat through waves of pain.

Knowing that his whole plan hung in the balance, Brian's eyes narrowed in anger. Pulling the pistol from his belt he pressed the barrel into Brodie's face. "See how you fuckers always underestimate me? Oh, that Brian Dix, he's not capable of putting together a workable plan, he's a mad dog, he's unstable, he's a fucking mentalist." Brian's nostrils flared in fury, his eyes blood-red as a violent temper eruption threatened to overwhelm his self-control. "You, Doherty, all those fuckers back home, you don't give me fucking credit." He squeezed the trigger almost all the way back before abruptly ripping the barrel away from Brodie's head. He let out a protracted whine of frustration not unlike a child's tantrum. He repeatedly hit himself in the face with the heel of the gun.

"Son, you are not firing on all cylinders for sure. If you think you're gonna get me in that car, you're crazier than a Bullbat."

"Oh you will get in the car Brodie," Brian threatened, "otherwise you can just lay there and imagine what I'm going to be doing to the sweet Tarina!"

Brodie's voice dropped to a whisper as he allowed Brian to drag him into the passenger side of the car. "You touch my girl and you'd better put an extra bullet in my skull when you're done boy 'cause I'm gonna be looking to kill you twice."

"Queue's forming on the right sir, so it is," Brian replied sarcastically, shoving the pistol back into his waistband. "Now if you don't mind, I like a little peace and quiet while I drive." With that he wrapped the gaffer tape around Brodie's mouth.

## CHAPTER SEVENTY THREE

**The gates of hell**

They drove to a deserted commercial compound in the industrial rust land of East Waco. Inside the perimeter were old storage units, mostly neglected and abandoned. Brian had chosen one that still had a padlock in place, although entry was easy through a couple of loose tin panels. He dragged Brodie from the car and into the shed. Brodie could hear Tarina's soft whimpers; his heart felt near to breaking point.

Propping his incapacitated captive against an upright, Brian switched on a battery lantern.

The structure had a sloping corrugated steel roof with wooden pillars supporting it from the ground some ten feet apart. Joining the pillars to the roof timbers were two upright supports arranged either side of the pillar, forming a 'Y' shape.

Tarina's wrists were bound to these uprights with gaffer tape; she had more tape around her throat, mouth and around her waist. A length of timber had been crudely but effectively secured to the bottom of the pillar and her ankles were taped to this with her legs spread as wide as they could physically go. She was naked; naked and crucified.

"Now I know that you're as strong as a fucking ox and that you're going to hold out for hours no matter what kind of injuries I inflict on you, so I'm going to save you all that suffering." Brian reached into his waistband and brandished the handgun again. "Now I *am* going to kill you big man, so I am. You were quite willing to kill me on behalf of that bastard Doherty, weren't you? Kill you? Oh yes, that's a done deal. Now then, you can save your lady-love a lot of suffering if you tell me where they're keeping Natasha. If you tell me, I'll let her go and I'll end your suffering quickly, with a bullet to the temple." He ripped the gaffer tape from Brodie's mouth.

"Tarina, I love you honey, stay strong," Brodie shouted the moment his mouth was free.

"Shut up!" Brian shouted, hitting Brodie a savage blow in the face from the stock of the gun.

Tarina's muffled moans increased in volume and tempo.

Brodie shook his head, shook off the blow. The implications were too great. His love for Tarina was unconditional but he had never betrayed his word. He knew he would have to give Brian information; this was his opportunity to deliver Brian the false location, but it would need to be believable.

"You fucking coward Dix, always the soft target with you ain't it. You're just too scared to face up to a man, even when he can't fight back." Brodie was trying to rile him. "What's your fucking problem Dix? Your little weiner don't work, is that it? Can't get it up? Did you wanna fuck your own mommy, is that what's screwed you up? Was mommy always on her back with her legs apart, too busy to mind her little boy?" he derided. "Was that it Dix? You didn't get to suck teet coz they was always busy, huh?"

It didn't work. Whatever had sparked Brian's earlier loss of discipline was not about to occur again. He was still completely in control.

"OK Brodie," Brian laughed. "We're in no hurry so I'll give you your chance."

Picking up a length of steel pipe from the ground, he proceeded to beat his captive around the arms and torso, slowly and methodically. He avoided blows to Brodie's head to ensure he remained conscious. Leaving the best till last, he stood back and swung the bar with all his might, bringing the weapon down onto the mangled mess which was Brodie's legs. Brodie let out a blood-curdling scream and fainted.

A cup of water to the face brought him back to consciousness, back to hell. In his subconscious, he knew he couldn't take much more punishment; it was time to deliver the address, send Brian into the jaws of the trap.

"Well big man, had enough yet? You ready to spill the beans?" Brian taunted.

Brodie's head was slumped forward on his chest and he nodded, barely perceptibly.

"So, where is she then?" Don't you be thinking of fucking me over, otherwise I'll be straight back here to slit that bitch's throat." He gestured towards Tarina.

"Let Tarina go first."

"Uh, I have considered your generous offer but I must decline. Now come on Brodie, you saw what I did to that slut Tammy and that was just for fun. Now I'm motivated!"

Brodie paused for a while, collecting his thoughts. He knew that Brian would carry out his threats. Tarina's only chance for survival would be to send Brian into the jaws of the trap. He hoped he could be convincing enough.

"She's been moved to a nursing home. Llano, Birmingham Avenue, don't know the name of the place, that's where she's at." Brodie's head slumped forward again, his energy and resolve seemingly spent.

"Good, good. Well done you!" Brian taunted, clapping his hands in mock congratulations. He pulled the automatic pistol from his belt and shoved it in Brodie's face. "You'll be wanting me to send you to the big Harley shop in the sky now then huh? Let the little lady be on her way, right?"

Brodie nodded, this time energetically.

Tarina's sobs became more audible.

Brian briefly left the shed, returning after a few short minutes with the roll of gaffer tape.

Wrapping several turns around Brodie's mouth Brian said, "See, I knew I wouldn't get the truth from you straight off. You took that beating for nothing. Now I don't want to hear a peep out of you. I don't want you to tell me anything at all; no lies, no truths, no pleading, no begging, nothing. There'll be plenty of time for that later. Right now, you just sit back and be entertained."

He walked over to Tarina. Stooping down between her legs he put the gun down on the ground and picked up an ugly looking rusty metal implement. "Look at what I found just lying in the dirt earlier. Now why would somebody throw away such a handsome looking tool?" Stepping up slowly, he ran the massive, industrial Mole grips up the girl's slender, perfectly smooth thigh, pausing briefly at the valley of her sex, pushing the tool gently against her sensitive skin so that she could feel the kiss of the cold decaying metal before running them up her belly towards her perfect breasts.

Brodie was straining against the tape around his torso and wrists, pulling with all his substantial strength, willing the tape to give, even just slightly.

"Now don't you struggle my friend, just watch," Brian teased. "This one's on account, just so you know I mean what I say, so to speak." He opened the handles of the decrepit tool slowly, letting the tension build. "See that's what you get when you buy quality tools; all this dirt and filth and yet they still work a treat." He screwed the knurled knob on the back of the grips down tight so that the jaws would lock, and then some.

Brian gently lifted Tarina's left breast with his free hand, pinching the nipple. It hardened to his touch. Tarina's face flushed with the shame of her body's involuntary reaction. She glanced across at Brodie, her eyes struggling to convey her remorse.

"Look at those perfect buds," Brian taunted. "Such symmetry. Do all you Latino girls have such perfect breasts? Hey ho, not for long though." He held the angry, rusty metal implement up to Tarina's gaze like a tempting, tasty dish. Her eyes bulged with fear and impotency.

Brian Dix opened the jaws of the grips as wide as they would go and placed them around the still firm nipple of Tarina's left breast. Then without hesitation he closed the jaws.

Like a grape in a nutcracker the nipple was crushed, destroyed.

The stifled scream from Brodie's throat brought a smile of satisfaction to Brian's face.

Tarina did not faint or lose consciousness, she just whimpered into her gag, convulsing in agony as the pain pulsed through her chest with every beat of her heart. Brian left the massive Mole grips hanging from the flap of ruined breast tissue.

He returned to his other captive. Brodie was dripping sweat from the futile exertion he was placing on his restrained muscles. His eyes were bloodshot, stinging from his tears.

"Now my friend, when I take the gag off don't waste my time or her body parts cursing and threatening. Your situation is dire, and you're not stupid. You can see that you can't get away without outside help, and that's unlikely, so *now* you tell me where the delightful Natasha *really* is, and I'll be on my way. Otherwise, the 'now not quite so lovely' Tarina will never know the joys of breastfeeding, and that's just for starters. I know of a few other things which would prefer not to be introduced to Mr Mole Grips!"

Brian wiggled his tongue obscenely between the vee of the two longest fingers of his good hand, conveying his meaning in unmistakable terms.

"Are you Jewish Brodie? The Jews have a ceremony they perform on baby boys. They ritualise snipping the end of a boy's ding-a-ling off. Girls don't exactly have a winkle to cut, but they do have a little man in a boat." Brian balled the end of his tongue and pretended to attach imaginary Mole grips to it. "Want to see my take on giving girls the snip Brodie? It's just like pulling teeth!"

That was the final straw for Brodie; his spirit was broken. He couldn't allow this monster to do his beloved Tarina further harm, not for the sake of strangers. With the gag removed, he sang like a canary.

Brodie was a broken man; he truthfully answered Brian's questions and when he hesitated Brian would wander back over to Tarina and tug on the

Mole grips. Her muffled cries were all it took to moisten his vocal chords again.

Brian strolled back over to where he had put down the pistol. "Now I know I said I would put a bullet between your eyes Brodie, but you know what? I can't spare the bullets."

"Let Tarina go, please Irish, she's an innocent. You've got what you wanted," he pleaded now, all bravado and machismo gone, pleading for the life of the woman he loved.

"Relax my buck. I'm not going to kill her," he laughed. "No, *I'm* not going to kill her. You see Brodie, overnight this area becomes a haven for scumbags and druggies. They've long since abandoned this shed 'cause there's nothing left in here to steal. I'm going to give her 'Hobson's choice'. I'll take off the gag, she can keep shtum and no-one will come to let her out and she'll die of thirst in a few days, or she can sing out at the top of her voice." Brian lent his evil leering face in, close to Brodie's, further emphasising his menace. "I've seen some nice big black gang bangers hanging around this compound most nights. She may get lucky. She may be discovered by a man out walking his dog, a man who buys his mum a card on mother's day. I don't think so though. She's all tied up, naked, spread-eagled and available. This is a shit hole in a really shitty part of a shitty town, and let's face facts, she does look very, very sexy, even with a Mole wrench hanging from her titty. I wouldn't say her odds are great."

"You fucking inhuman bastard," Brodie whispered, defeated.

Brian bent over and retrieved the length of construction steel. "Now you'll appreciate this, my friend, you Texans like a ballgame don't you?" He shouldered the pole and swung a few times imitating a baseball player. "Strike one, strike two." He shouldered the pole once more and asked Brodie seriously, "Now what do they call it when you deliberately hit a short ball? When you make out you're going to swing, but instead you just touch the ball down?"

"Go to hell you sadistic bastard."

"Come now, don't be rude." Brian walked over to Tarina and tapped a couple of times gently on the Mole grips. She winced and pulled back, causing the grips to swing wildly from the tortured flesh. Tarina fainted.

"A bunt," Brodie called out, dejected, resigned to his fate. "It's called a bunt."

"That's the one," Brian mocked. "Let's see if I get this right," he said, and swung the iron pole full force into Brodie's head. "Ooops! Damn, I hit a home run! See that's always been my trouble, no self-restraint."

Brian dropped the iron pole and walked over to Tarina to retrieve his gun. He carefully, almost tenderly, removed the tape from her mouth, studying her full ruby-red lips. He inclined her head and placed his open mouth on hers. "Mmm, you do taste good honey, I can see the attraction." Tarina remained in a faint.

"Hey wake up," Brian growled. When the girl didn't stir, he grasped the handles of the Mole wrench and tugged down, hard. Tarina woke up abruptly and screamed.

"That's better. Now then my lovely, your boyfriend is hurt bad, it's up to you to save him. I'm off now, but when I'm gone, you have my permission to scream the place down. Get him some help!"

With that Brian left the shed, chuckling to himself as if to some private joke. He sat behind the wheel of the Camaro with the window down, waiting. He heard the girl's first scream. "That'll bring the rats a scurrying!" With a smile he fired up the engine and screeched out of the compound.

As the tail lights faded into the distance the shadows emerged, took form and headed for the sound of the woman's screams like rats towards the Pied Piper.

## CHAPTER SEVENTY FOUR

**Incident**

Pump Four of the Waco Fire Department were returning from a hoax shout in the Elk Road area of East Waco when one of the fire-fighters saw a number of hooded youths run out of the gates of a disused industrial complex. A dull orange glow was emanating from one of the units.

The pump was primed. A quick call to control confirmed the address and alerted the Waco Police Department. The pump was authorised to attend the fire.

The fire had not become established and once the doors had been ripped open with bolt croppers it was quickly extinguished. The lead fire-fighter removed his helmet. He heard a faint sobbing from the corner.

"Jesus H Christ!"

He quickly registered what he saw and raised the two way radio to his mouth.

"Pump Four to sector eight control."

"Sector eight control, go ahead Pump Four."

"Pump Four, ten-fifty-two required at this twenty, EMS code three response stat. IC one female, signal thirty-one, serious injuries."

"Sector eight control copy Pump Four, dispatching ambulance now, EMS code three."

The fire-fighter cut the tape around Tarina's ankles, then reached up and cut the tape holding her to the cross. As she fell forward across the fire-fighter's shoulders the Mole wrench was pulled, causing her to scream out in pain. He carried her outside the building and laid her on the floor.

"Can we get a blanket over here?" he called to the other fire-fighters who were busy winding up hoses and clearing the equipment.

"I'm sorry honey, we need to wait for the paramedics before we touch anything. With Tarina laid out on the floor he made a quick sweep of her with his torch. Her vital signs were OK. She had extensive bruising around her face and body. Her lips were bleeding and swollen. Her genital area was bruised and lacerated, caked with blood and body fluids. Despite an overwhelming feeling of compassion he knew better than to try to clean her up; it was evidence.

Her breast with the wrench still attached was purple from bruising. The crushed tissue inside the jaws was black. The fire-fighter had done a stint with mountain rescue; he knew from experience that it had gone too long without a blood supply to be sustainable. He was concerned now that if he removed the wrench she may get an infection or suffer significant blood loss. Her other breast had not completely escaped attention, it too was purple from bruising, the skin filled with tiny burst blood vessels making it appear to be criss-crossed with hundreds of tiny cuts. The fire-fighter guessed it to be the result of repeated slapping. The thought of the torture this poor girl had endured brought the bile up to the man's throat. He had a daughter at home not much younger than her.

Tarina sobbed and tried to prop herself on her elbows.

"Keep still honey, the paramedics will be here soon, they'll take good care of you."

She couldn't speak; her lips and gums were too swollen. She grabbed the man's leg, pointed at the shed with a look of urgency, and then collapsed.

The fire-fighter gestured to one of his colleagues. "Go take another sweep of the shed, she seems real anxious about something."

Two of the firemen walked into the building. Their powerful hand lamps lit up the smokey interior.

"Good God almighty, we got another one in here."

The two men dropped their torches and dragged Brodie from the still smoking building. Feeling for a pulse, the fireman looked over to the lead fire-fighter and shouted, "Call in a ten-seventy-nine."

This was the code in the Waco district to request the coroner's attendance.

The paramedics were next on the scene. An approaching police cruiser could be heard off in the distance.

"You'll be OK now honey, soon have you safe and sound in a nice warm bed, you'll be OK now."

As the ambulance crew busied themselves with securing Tarina on to the stretcher and into the ambulance, the paramedic moved over to Brodie.

"This one the ten-seventy-nine?"

"Yea, can't feel any vitals. The way his head's stoved in I should think he died instantly," the fire-fighter who'd dragged Brodie out replied.

The paramedic did a vitals sweep of Brodie for the record.

"Holy shit, he's got a pulse."

The spot where Brodie lay immediately became a hive of activity as further paramedics rushed across from the ambulance with breathing apparatus, drips and crash equipment.

Still in charge of the scene, the lead fire-fighter reacted instinctively. "Pump Four, sector eight control copy?"

"Sector eight control, go ahead Pump Four."

"Pump Four, sector eight control, we have a further signal sixteen. Repeat, a second signal sixteen at this twenty. Signal thirty-three code four. Air evac required. Sector eight control copy?"

"Sector eight control, copy that Pump Four, second casualty, EMS air evac advised. What is the nature of medical emergency Pump Four?"

"Pump Four, control. IC one male, mid-forties, severe head trauma, trauma to torso and legs. Severe lacerations to legs. Severe blood loss and possible smoke inhalation. Paramedics attending. Over.

"Sector eight control, Pump Four, be advised ETA for EMS air evac eight minutes."

"Pump Four, sector eight control, understood, out."

As the police cruiser screeched to a halt on the shale road Brodie's life hung in the lap of the gods.

## CHAPTER SEVENTY FIVE

**Marital**

Jimbo and Goose pulled up outside the Romero Hotel. Goose had plumped for using the reliable Sporty, surmising that the pimp mobile was just a little too conspicuous.

Once booked in, the boys were busy piling up the beer and provisions they felt would be necessary for the down time between stake-out duty.

"Budweiser, Goose? Oh for mercy's sake! I weigh over 18 stone, I'm going to be pissing rivers before this shit gets me mellow."

"Oh bugger, bollocks and bum holes Jimbo. This is a serious assignment. Do you never stop thinking about getting pissed?" He continued piling the cans of Bud into the fridge.

"They're bloody boys' beers. Couldn't you have found something a little more substantial?"

"Jimbo! Jesus Christ man! What does it take for heaven's sake? We're in a war zone. Can you be serious for just a few days?"

"Nothing's going to kick off for a few days though is it? It's going to take twat face more than a few days to get wind of the nursing home for sure. In that time I'll have got through those bloody cans of piss, and spent most of my time in the kharzi."

"We're going to be spending most of our time in the nursing home anyway; you'll have to be cold stone sober when we're over there. You're not watching my back through bloodshot eyes."

## Bittersweet Humiliation

Goose was rapidly losing patience with his petulant buddy.

"I won't be watching your back; I'll be perched on the throne spraying fizzy brown lemonade over my shoes if I drink that crap you've brought in."

"Aargh... you... you... you're just impossible!" Goose threw the last of the tinnies into the fridge and slammed the door.

Jimbo smiled. He knew he riled his buddy up but he also knew it stopped Goose from getting all stressed and paranoid about the impending action. It was a mood stabilising ploy, and he had the balance pretty well off pat.

Brushing past Goose he opened the fridge and took out a beer. Pulling the ring pull, he put the tin to his lips and drained it in one hit before scowling at Goose and retiring to the bathroom.

"Aaargh!" Goose screamed. "God give me strength."

Jimbo had his hand between his teeth, biting down hard to stifle the laughter.

"Right c'mon, I can't take any more, let's go back down the store and daddy will let you choose your own beverages."

Jimbo flushed the loo and opened the door a crack before whispering in a high pitched voice, "I want an ice cream too!"

Goose kicked the door in and grabbed the giant by the throat, as if he would throttle him.

Jimbo was laughing so hard he couldn't defend himself. Pretty soon the two of them were prostrate on the floor in fits of laughter.

"C'mon you muppet," Jimbo joked. "Let's nip back down the store and get ourselves some proper provisions."

Hotel residents in the lobby were treated to a fading conversation like that of a bickering old married couple as the two bikers walked briskly out of the foyer.

"You didn't get me any Pringles," Jimbo whinged.

"You didn't ask for Pringles!"

"I want root beer and Dr Pepper."

"What for, you've got plenty of soft drinks!"

"For the Pringles. You've got to have Dr Pepper and root beer with Pringles!"

"Jimbo, sometimes I swear, you're such a cock, I don't know why I married you!"

"I have great tits!"

"You're a fucking great tit," Goose cussed, laughing and shaking his head in equal measures.

For the sake of appearances, Neil had secured a separate family suite in the Romero Hotel. The children would be booked in using their own names although they would stay in the relative safe haven of Warren's ranch. If Brian were to check the hotel register he would expect the kids to be nearby. He shouldn't recognise Jimbo or Goose so it was OK for them to just come and go like part of the general public. It was hoped that with the heightened security and Neil's regular comings and goings, Brian would think Natasha was indeed at the home and fall into the trap.

## CHAPTER SEVENTY SIX

**Attack**

Brian was back doing what he did best: Blitzkrieg. In the front door, act, react, fluidity. Planning was not one of his great strengths. Blessed with the reactions and feral wits of a wildcat, his psychotic mind was ideally suited to concentrating, to focusing entirely on the one big job in hand. So much so he had to remind himself to eat, drink and defecate.

He was hiding out in an empty basement boiler room. As he exited he passed a joke shop selling, amongst other tat, novelty hats. Brian helped himself to a baseball cap bearing the slogan, 'Redneck and proud', complete with sewn in mullet hairstyle. He tried the cap on, backwards, so the long hair hung over his face like curtains. He parted the hair, pushing it back behind his ears. A distraction was all he needed; it would do.

Next stop was a pool supplies shop. In the dumpster behind the shop he found just what he was after; some discarded hose and a few empty sodium hypochlorite tubs, emblazoned with a convincing picture of a bikini clad babe in a glorious blue pool and the words 'Pool Chlorine' in big letters.

He threw his acquisitions into the Camaro and headed out onto the highway.

He was headed for Marble Falls.

## CHAPTER SEVENTY SEVEN

**Parting**

Neil collected all the things he would need to have with him while he was staying away. Warren's wife, Nell, had established a routine with the children and Neil knew that they would be well looked after in his absence. Leaving them alone was the last thing he wanted to do, but he knew they needed to take the initiative. They couldn't just keep waiting for Brian's next move. He was a hunted man and he was clever. Neil felt sure that if they didn't bring the fight to him, he might just find a way through their defences.

Last stop was to say goodbye to Natasha.

Della was living in the ranch now, looking after Natasha twenty-four-seven. Neil had suggested the arrangement and in return he would sponsor her through medical school where she would have the chance to qualify as a doctor. Della had readily agreed.

"Hi Della, how's my girl?"

"You know what Neil? I see a definite change in her. She is calming down. Her eyes don't look so haunted. Mrs Bateson brought the children in to see her. I swear for a second I thought she smiled."

"That's marvellous news Della. I see what you're getting at. The tension seems to be leaving her. She looked all coiled up like a spring before, now she seems to be almost relaxed."

"She loves it when you visit. You know, I swear it won't be long before she comes back."

"Hi honey," Neil whispered, stroking the back of Natasha's hand. "Honey, I've got to take off for a little while, I've some important business to attend to. You'll be fine here. Warren will be here to take care of you, and so will Della. Nell will look in on you every day; she'll bring the kids by to see you. I'll be back soon, and then we can go home and get back to normal, put all this behind us. You'll see, we'll put all the bad and the hurt behind us and get back to the life we loved."

Natasha's face remained impassive, expressionless. Neil had to stifle a choke as he gazed into those lifeless eyes. How he wanted to tell her that Brian was gone. How he wished for that to be true.

His eyes filled with tears. Della put a hand on his shoulder to comfort him and he cupped her hand with his, then lifted it away and left the room.

It was time to put his game face on. There was no room for emotion where he was going.

Just as he was preparing to leave, the phone rang. Neil overheard Warren talking; the tone sounded urgent, important. Neil thought he'd better stick around, see what was up.

As he put the phone down, Warren turned to Neil.

"It's Brodie, he's in the hospital in Waco. He's been kidnapped and tortured. He's fighting for his life!"

## CHAPTER SEVENTY EIGHT

**False twenty**

Neil drove like a maniac to the nursing home. He hadn't time to drive to Waco and visit Brodie. From what he knew of the man, he was confident that Brodie would have set the trap.

Brian would be on his way!

He called into the Romero Hotel. Goose and Jimbo weren't in their room. *Damn,* he thought. He hadn't time to look for them; he had to be in position when Brian came. On a whim, he snatched up the keys to the Sportster. He quickly scribbled a note to the boys, telling them to hightail it across to the nursing home on their return.

The whole wing of the nursing home, supposedly 'home' to Natasha, had been cleared of all civilian personnel. In their place were CIA men, hand-picked representatives from the Sheriff's Department and some private detectives. Neil was to be the decoy. His job was to be visible so that Brian would know where to go, where he could be cornered and trapped.

As he ran into the reception area, he was called over by the private dick manning the reception phone.

"Mr Curland, got a lady on the phone here, she's pretty incoherent, she'll speak to you and no-one else."

"Hello, Neil Curland."

"Neil?" the voice enquired. The woman sounded weak and laboured.

"Yes, this is Neil. What do you want?"

## Bittersweet Humiliation

"This is Tarina, Brodie's girlfriend. He just about did for Brodie, Neil."

"I'm so sorry to hear that Tarina. I'm tied up here at the moment, but you tell Brodie, we'll be over just as soon as we can. We'll do anything possible to help him."

"I can't tell him anything Neil, he's hanging by a thread. He told him Neil, told him where she is. He couldn't help himself, he had to tell."

"Do you know what he said Tarina? Did Brodie set him up for us?"

The pause at the end of the line seemed to last an age. "No… No he didn't, he tried, but it was all too much. That animal broke him Neil. He told him, he told him for real, told him everything!"

Neil Curland's heart missed a beat. His throat constricted as her words hit home.

Neil crashed the receiver back down and barked to the detective, "Get Mr Bateson on the phone, tell him Brian knows where she is. Tell him Brian's on his way there *now!*"

Neil ran across the road, instinctively deciding to take the Sportster rather than the bog slow station wagon.

## CHAPTER SEVENTY NINE

**Absent minded**

The shopping trip had taken nearly an hour. When the boys returned to the Romero Hotel they let themselves back into the room and dumped the big box of provisions down on the table, right on top of the note from Neil.

Goose busied himself with the task of unpacking the box and stashing the goods in their respective lockers while Jimbo went back for one of his many visits to the loo to jettison some of his healthy diet of junk food.

Goose's attention was suddenly attracted to the ashtray which contained the ignition keys from Jimbo's Panhead Harley.

"Where's the keys to the Sporty?" he asked, concerned.

"I dunno. You didn't go and leave them in the ignition again did you, like you're always doing back home?"

"Oh bollocks," Goose cursed and quickly exited the room, making for the elevator.

"You'll be bloody lucky mate, this is America not bloody Wisbech. You can expect a thank you note!" Jimbo shouted after him.

The elevator was down on the ground floor. Goose decided he would be quicker using the stairs and made for the stairwell.

Taking the steps two and three at a time, he was on his way out of the foyer five minutes after leaving the room.

As he left the hotel, the feeling of impending dread made him quicken his step.

Turning the corner of the building, he was in near full flight mode when he ran headlong into Neil.

"Where's Jimbo?"

"He's up in the room; we just got back from shopping for supplies."

"Didn't you see my note?"

"What note?"

"We don't have time for this, Brian's after Natasha. Quickly, jump on."

Neil mounted the front seat, fired up the Harley and manhandled the bike into an upright position. Without further explanation, Goose jumped on the pillion seat.

With a screech of burning rubber on tortured asphalt, Neil was on the move before Warren had even picked up the phone.

## CHAPTER EIGHTY

**Killer on the loose**

The blue Camaro pulled up at the Bateson Ranch gates.

The driver was wearing a Walkman and singing some surfer song at the top of his voice. As one of the two security guards at the gate approached him, the driver pulled one of the buds from his ear and called, "Pool guy!"

Brian reached to the seat beside him and the guard reacted swiftly, his hand on his firearm.

"Relax dude," Brian called out, producing the tub of chlorine by way of credentials. "Don't have a coronary. I'm just here to clean the pool. I come by every month, just ask the lady of the house."

The guard relaxed slightly and turned to speak to the other guard. Brian got his first break; the second guard jumped the gun and pressed the button to open the electric gates. It was the mistake Brian needed. In the seconds of confusion which followed, the muzzle on his silenced handgun flashed twice. Two undramatic pops were all that could be heard. Nevertheless, at that precise moment, another two hearts stopped beating at the hands of Brian Dix.

The guard in the CCTV room was staring at the coffee cup perched on the corner of his desk. He had forgotten he'd made himself a drink and was trying to guess whether it still retained enough temperature before committing himself to touching the cup and knowing for sure. It was one of those stupid games you played when it was your job to sit and wait for something to happen. His attention had been diverted away from the monitors for no more than a minute. He touched the coffee cup. "Goddamn it, cold."

He glanced back up at the bank of monitors, his gaze going from the left side of the display to the right as was customary.

Had the monitors been set in a dedicated curved display, the action at the gatehouse may have elicited a reaction from his peripheral vision. Unfortunately, the monitors at the Bateson Ranch had been added gradually over time in the absence of a significant security risk. They were arranged in a linear fashion with the gatehouse monitor the furthest away from the man's natural field of vision. As he focused on the last monitor in the array, he realised something was wrong. Before he had even acknowledged the bodies of his comrades from the gatehouse lying in the driveway his training kicked in and his hand hovered over the alarm button. Suddenly he was kicked in the back. His hand hung suspended over the monitors, the alarm button out of his reach. A random thought pervaded his brain, he questioned what he had eaten to have given him such severe heartburn, and why, he wondered, had he stopped breathing?

Brian caught hold of the guard's chair, wheeled him backwards away from the monitors, then pushed chair and inert occupant violently to the side of the room, sending the dead guard sprawling onto the floor with the chair on top of him.

Laying the still smoking handgun on the desk, he scanned the monitors. Each room shown on the screens had a digital signature emblazoned across the base. The one he was interested in had the words, 'Stairwell B bedroom 3' written across the bottom in fifty hertz flickering intensity. It was the room containing the vulnerable Natasha. Glancing between the array of monitors gave him a snapshot of the layout of the ranch. Not exactly a route planner, but a pretty good clue. Not wishing to lose the advantage, he quickly reloaded the gun and ran across the courtyard to the entrance of the ranch. A startled security guard was caught behind the patio doors. As he reached into his shoulder holster the first round of hot metal pierced clean through the door glass and dropped the guard on to his back. The second round shattered the toughened glass which fell to the ground like a frozen waterfall. Before the guard had drawn his last breath, Brian was through the redundant door frame and up the staircase.

## CHAPTER EIGHTY ONE

**Counter attack**

Neil gunned the engine of the Harley, wringing every last revolution from the motor as he slewed the bike sideways through the open gates of the Bateson Ranch. The bike lurched violently as he attempted to lift the heavy front wheel to climb the steps of the patio, almost throwing him over the handlebars. The sheer tempo carried him up the steps and through the patio doors. A trials bike, even perhaps a lighter British twin, would have responded to Neil's command to climb the giant oak staircase, but a heavy Harley, two up? The bike gave him everything it had to give, finally stopping dead at the top of the stairs, and tossing Neil over the handlebars like a rag doll. He flew through the air for no more than a fraction of a second; time enough to register the twisted evil face of his nemesis moving in on his prey! Neil landed with a sickening crunch on the landing. His right leg took the brunt of the impact and broke beneath him. He knew the advantage of surprise would last but precious seconds. Still charged with the energy of momentum, he hurled himself at Brian, sending him crashing through the door of Natasha's room. Hearing the deafening commotion, Della had grabbed the only weapon she had agreed to have in the room with Natasha – a baseball bat. The door hit Della square in the face, catapulting her across the room, knocked out cold. Natasha retreated into the corner of the room and crouched on the floor, gently swaying from side to side.

The gun had been knocked from Brian's grasp. He scanned quickly, saw the baseball bat and grabbed it up.

Like a scene from one of his action movies, Warren came out of nowhere and hurled his large frame through the doorway, attempting to level an enormous elephant gun as his stampede left him momentarily off balance.

Brian was too quick for him. Spinning on the balls of his feet he hit Warren squarely in the kneecaps with the baseball bat, sending him crashing to the ground next to the frozen figure of Natasha, knocking the wind out of him and pinning the huge weapon under his body.

Realising that Warren was out of the game, Brian hurled his full weight onto Neil and straddled his torso, pinning his twisted broken leg below his body, trapping him.

Too slowly, he drew the assault knife from his tac vest, giving the wounded Neil time to grab his wrists in a desperate struggle to prevent him pressing home his advantage.

Brian brought all his strength to bear; attempting to manoeuvre the assault weapon down towards Neil's chest.

Sweat ran from Brian's face, hovering inches above Neil's. Salty venom ran between the stubble on the hate contorted features, dripping into Neil's eyes and impairing his vision, blurring what could well be the last images he would see in this life.

Pain and blood loss were conspiring to rob Neil of his strength and stamina. He was fighting a losing battle to keep his hate crazed opponent from pushing the blade into his chest and sealing his fate.

Inside Natasha's head something had begun to stir. It was like the fleeting, random memories of a recent dream state had begun to solidify, to concur. Thoughts, previously crashing around like particles in a vortex, were beginning to merge into coherent sentences; awareness was creeping through the fog in her head.

A voice inside her tortured mind was screaming at her to take charge, to take back her world, to fight back for her life and her family.

She could see the real world outside of the safe dark place she had created for herself within. Her eyes were open but the view she observed was that of a mere portal at the end of a long winding tunnel. Through that tiny pinprick of vision she could see the source of all evil, poised to destroy everything she once held dear, poised to destroy any chance she would have of a future, condemning her to the darkness of the 'safe place' for eternity.

With all the strength she possessed she strove to reach the portal, to break back into the real world.

Peripheral vision returned to Natasha like the first celluloid frames of an old silent cine film. With it, instant comprehension.

Warren lay on his stomach; he was trying to lift himself off the floor using his arms as his legs were rendered useless by the injury to his knees. The pain from his shattered limbs was excruciating, causing him to temporarily lose consciousness. The huge gun lay on the floor beneath him, trapped. Natasha reached out, gripping the barrel. She tried to pull the gun free.

"Time to die Soldier Boy," Brian panted, as the tip of the knife found a gap between Neil's ribs.

## CHAPTER EIGHTY TWO

**Reinforcements**

As the Harley had come to an abrupt halt at the top of the stairs, Goose had been thrown forward and caught his groin on the handlebars, throwing his head forward and breaking his pelvis and collarbone with a single crack. The kinetic energy stored in the bike's forks from the mad forward charge recoiled and the bike lurched backwards. Its weight took it out over the destroyed banister rail and down to the floor below, with Goose still caught up with it.

As his helmetless head had contacted the front mudguard he had been momentarily knocked unconscious. Landing heavily on the downstairs floor his left wrist had shattered on the marble surface, dissipating the force of the fall and protecting his vulnerable head from more serious damage. Regaining consciousness at the foot of the stairs, Goose was in agony. A quick situation report told him that his left hand, right arm and left leg were as good as useless. He knew that he must somehow transport his broken body up the stairs to join the fray. Neil and Natasha needed him.

Despite the debilitating pain from his injuries, he bit down and slithered up the stairs, propelling himself from step to step with a sideways motion of his left elbow and right leg.

He reached the open doorway in the nick of time.

From his vantage point flat on the floor, Goose could see the trapped hunting rifle and could see what Natasha was trying to do. With all the strength he could muster from his broken body he pushed with his good right leg against Warren's torso, rolling the heavy man over and freeing the pinned weapon.

## CHAPTER EIGHTY THREE

**Phoenix**

Something registered in Brian's peripheral vision. He was momentarily distracted. A sardonic smile flickered across his face.

Neil saw the flash reflected in Brian's eyes and smelt the cordite charge in the air before he heard the retort of Warren's massive hunting gun.

Brian's grip on the knife suddenly loosened; the weight of him bearing down lessened. His final image of Natasha's revenge was erased from his retinas by the enormous destructive power of the weapon.

The headless torso remained in its prone position over Neil in a macabre freeze-frame.

"Before I forget, Tammy says hello," Neil whispered as he pushed the erect corpse to the floor.

"Neil." Natasha's voice was little more than a horse croak. "Neil, are you OK?"

"I'm OK darling, thanks to you. Oh my God, are you back? Are you really back?"

"I'm back Neil." She started to sob. "I want to live Neil, I want my life back. I want my family back!"

"Is Warren OK?" Neil asked, concerned for their friend.

Warren replied in his own indomitable way, "I'm OK Neil. That bastard was born sorry, he jumped on me with all four feet, smashed both my goddamn knees. Oww, goddamn, I am so sick, I'll have to get better before I can die. How 'bout you Neil? You bearing up?"

"My leg's pretty broken up too," Neil replied. Then borrowing a phrase from their Texan friend's vocabulary he said, "I'm as full of pains as an old window."

Warren let out a snort of laughter between grimaces.

"I'll make a Texan of you yet Neil." He painfully turned his head to Natasha. "Girl, you sure picked an opportune moment to come back to us! You saved our lives Natasha, all of us."

"Come over here, I need to hold you," Neil called out.

Natasha staggered over to him, collapsing across his chest. After months of inactivity the meagre energy in her muscles was quickly spent.

Neil stroked her hair and hugged her to him. "I love you Natasha. I'll never let you out of my sight again."

"I love you too Neil, promise me we can have our lives back now!"

"I promise you. This is a fresh start for us, from this day on, everything I do will be to make life better for you," Neil replied with deep sincerity in his words.

"Neil," Warren called out, "how we gonna raise the cavalry?"

"I don't know Warren; I don't think Natasha can stand up and *we're* both hobbled."

"That only leaves Brian," Warren smiled, in a gesture of impromptu graveyard humour.

Surveying the absolute carnage the now headless corpse had left in its wake, the numerous injured bodies lying scattered around the room, the tears welled up in Neil's eyes. Nervous tension threatened to destroy his resolve, to render him a blubbing, gibbering wreck. Instead, he threw his head back and laughed. The sound originated deep in his stomach. Warren joined him; more a release of nervous tension and pain than mirth, but nonetheless cathartic.

"Yes thanks guys, I'm OK as it happens. Most of the bones in my body are broken, but it's OK, I'm just glad to have been of service," Goose announced sarcastically.

"Goose, bugger! I forgot I had a passenger. Are you OK mate?"

"No mate, I'm all busted up. But you know what, I feel bloody marvellous, because that fucking worthless piece of shit has finally got his comeuppance!"

"Amen," Warren added.

Natasha was lying with her head on Neil's chest, fast asleep, mercifully oblivious to the inappropriate macho banter.

Stirrings from the corner of the room reminded them that they weren't alone.

"Ow my head, where am I?"

"Della! Are you OK honey?" Neil asked.

"I think so, apart from a goddamn banging headache!"

"Della, do you think you could be a love and get to the telephone in the next room and raise the alarm?"

Della looked at the headless corpse lying on the floor. "Who the hell is that? Ugh, gross, where's his head?" she asked, genuinely bewildered.

The whole situation had taken on a surreal quality. The sheer relief generated by the final demise of their, until recently, unassailable foe, created a feeling of euphoria which could only be dissipated by wholesome British humour.

"That, Della, was the headless *horsemen of the apocalypse,* otherwise known as the villain of the piece, Brian Dix. I'm delighted to say that it was my darling wife who facilitated the removal of said piece of scum's head. She's having a well-deserved sleep right now, but when she wakes up, it will give me great pleasure to introduce you to her."

"I know Della already," a drowsy Natasha croaked. "She's my friend."

## CHAPTER EIGHTY FOUR

**Healing**

Clearing up the mess the late Brian Dix left in his wake would require good fortune and time, plenty of time.

Neil's, Warren's and Goose's wounds were relatively straightforward. With the skills of the country's best orthopaedic surgeons they were all quickly on the mend.

Tarina's injuries were complicated. As predicted the damaged breast tissue wasn't viable and a secondary infection had necessitated further tissue removal as the surgeons fought to save her milk ducts and the rest of her breast.

Once again, Warren's Hollywood contacts proved invaluable. An eminent cosmetic surgeon had pioneered a ground-breaking procedure where erectile tissue was transferred by graft slowly from one area of the body to another. Using this process he was able to reconstruct a semi-functioning nipple to Tarina's breast, with inspirational tattoo shading courtesy of the best tattoo artist in the Southern States, who just happened to be an associate of Brodie's. Again with the passage of old Father Time to help mask the scarring, Tarina would one day be able to look at her body in the mirror without wincing.

The sexual attack had left her with a treatable venereal disease and severe trauma. Antibiotics and the counselling of her new friend Natasha, a woman who had been through far worse at the hands of the same antagonist, would see her through the worst.

Natasha made remarkable physical progress. The cosmetic restoration procedures she underwent whilst in surgery for her more serious injuries had been a great success. Neil had stressed the importance his wife placed on her smile, her immaculate teeth being her pride and joy. The results did not disappoint. Helping Tarina through the healing process yielded a positive therapeutic effect on Natasha's psychological recovery too.

After his recovery, Goose felt that the weather in Texas agreed with him and he decided to transfer his bank accounts stateside. He came to the conclusion that what was needed in his life, to ward off the evil spirit of depression, was constant stress and excitement. To this end he spoke at length with Warren and Neil about an idea of his to set up a detective agency. Again, the benevolent Warren would not be far away with a list of celebrity clients and temporary accommodation in the golf lodge to get him off the ground. With his exemplary skills in surveillance, success was assured.

After Natasha had explained to Neil the part that Goose had played in Brian's defeat, Neil felt he owed his friend a debt of gratitude which could never be repaid. Goose sat Neil down and explained to him what he was just about to do when Neil had phoned with the news of the kidnapping.

"So you see," he said, "in reality it's you who saved my life, so we'll call it quits."

Jimbo took his leave and flew home as soon as he was sure he wouldn't be missed. Goose's mum would be lonely in her big old house alone, and Jimbo was happy with his sedentary life. Sure, he would miss his best mucker, but England was home. He could always come back to visit and no doubt Goose would call upon his 'strong arm services' from time to time in his new profession.

## CHAPTER EIGHTY FIVE

### Ventures new

Brodie's recovery was nothing short of miraculous. It was a testament to what can be achieved when unlimited resources are made available from the get go. The second Brodie's plight had come to Warren's attention a phone call had seen him placed in the care of the States' foremost center for neurological medicine. In a procedure pioneered in Russia, Brodie's damaged brain was packed with ice before receiving treatment from the country's top neurosurgeon. Brodie's injuries were grave. Nevertheless, the surgeon's great skill and perhaps divine fortitude allowed him to survive. After a time he regained the power of speech and brevity to a level not far below his pre-injured wit. His injured legs did not fare so well. The vascular damage to his right leg was too severe. If this had been his only injury it may have been possible to repair some of the damage and perhaps save the leg or at least delay the inevitable. With the massive blood loss combined with his head injuries, the decision to amputate was the only option, and so it was that he lost his right leg, just above the knee. His left leg had a solid blood supply and was able to be saved for further procedures at a later date. Brodie's timely proposal of marriage to his girlfriend Tarina, just before she underwent the cosmetic surgeon's knife for the final time, had an overwhelmingly positive effect on her ebbing self-esteem, and gave him a valid reason to recover.

## Bittersweet Humiliation

Waco Slaves' MC Club charter required that their President rode his bike on a minimum number of outings. The charter did not allow for an armchair President. Such was the esteem in which Brodie was held that the founding chapter was petitioned to declare an exception, allowing Brodie to remain President while he recuperated.

"Have you decided what you're going to do Brodie?" Neil asked.

"Yea, I'm going to step down. Club don't need a crippled President and I don't need their pity."

"Shows just how much your guys respect you though pal," Neil pointed out.

"Yea, I know, I love my club, they're all good boys, but you know Neil, when you're boss of an outlaw club, you gotta be meaner and tougher than the next man. No, it's time for me to step down and take my leave; they'll let me walk away with honour this way. If I hang in there, I might let them down, then things wouldn't be so sweet."

"Do you think you'll be able to ride again?" Neil asked.

"Not on a solo, I don't think I'll get my balance back, not properly. Doc says there's damage to my inner ear, causes me to be a bit wobbly. No, with that and the leg, I can't see me on two wheels again."

Neil was deep in thought, considering how to help his friend.

"What about a trike?"

"A what?" Brodie questioned with a puzzled look on his face.

"A motor trike, a motorcycle based trike. We could trike your Glide!"

Brodie laughed,

"You gonna build me a little Servicar Neil?"

"Not a Servicar Brodie, I'm thinking more of a full blown triked, chopped hog, like on that film, 'Mad Max'."

Now it was Brodie's turn to have an epiphany.

"Neil, what about an offshoot from Copper Road Choppers? What about Copper Road Trikes?"

"By jingo, the man's a genius! Do you think there would be an audience for it?" Neil quickly interjected.

"Hey, I'm only thinking as far as building the goddamn things and already you've got a TV show lined up. Let's take one step at a time man. Hell, the US of A is a damn vast country, sure there's gotta be a hell of a lot of others in my position. Not just that, there's gotta be thousands of people who'd ride a trike just for fun."

"I reckon you're bang on the money there Brodie."

Neil contemplated the idea for a while before saying, "What do you think Brodie? Is that something you could organise?"

"What do you think Neil? I've been running a Harley business, a roadhouse and a motorcycle club for years. I reckon a trike shop would be like a holiday for me."

"Work it out then Brodie, do the math, then double everything, then double everything again. Remember, this isn't a new venture; we already have the capital and the track record. Got to think big from the off."

Brodie offered his hand to Neil for a robust 'biker' handshake.

"You got it Boss."

"Partner." Neil shook his hand. "I'm not looking for staff. You run the show, I'll bankroll it. You take a wage until the initial investment is paid off, then I'll take a cut of the profits and the rest is yours. I'll speak to Warren further down the line, see if there's another spin off TV show in it. Deal?"

"Yea, sounds to me like we got something. I'll get my business head on and start looking for premises, equipment etc. Get some costs worked out," Brodie replied.

"Let me have some figures when you have them, I'll telex my people in the UK and we'll make it happen."

## CHAPTER EIGHTY SIX

### The old routine

With the passage of time Natasha's old confidence was returning. It would be a slow uphill battle, but with Neil's love and support and the support of her family and friends she knew it was a battle she could win.

"Neil, I think I'd like to go back home soon," Natasha said.

"What about us staying in the States? You've changed your mind?"

"Right now, I think I'd like to be away from here. I just think I'd like to get back home, I don't know, see my mum, see your mum and dad again. It's been a long time. I want to go home, for a while at least. We can still change our minds and come back, but right now I need to get back to solid reality, feel the old familiar grass under my feet."

"You're right. I feel like I've been living from a suitcase for years. You're dead right; we need to go home, get the kids back in school and get back to some sort of a routine. I can still fly back and forth every couple of weeks to keep things moving forward on the business front. I'll give Janice a ring, get her to organise the house for our homecoming."

"Thank you Neil," Natasha said, sincerely.

"Darling, I'll go anywhere in the world to be with you, anywhere!"

"Thank you Neil. I love you!"

"I love you too Natasha, more than I love life itself."

## Bittersweet Humiliation

Despite all the hurt and terrible suffering she'd endured, Natasha could feel the warmth returning to her soul. Brian was gone. Now the past could finally be laid to rest.

# EPILOGUE

## A time of reckoning

Following Natasha's information, the incriminating evidence of the video tapes and considerable pressure from Warren's CIA friends, a number of individuals were able to be located and brought to justice. Michael and Janine were no bother to track down and arrest. Balaclava and the butcher referred to as 'the vet' proved more elusive and remained at large. The barn where Natasha was held captive was never found; they simply had nothing to go on. Natasha remembered well the role played by Aiden, but in the end decided that without his intervention, self-serving though it was, she would have probably wound up dead. She decided to leave him to his own fate.

The final wrong which required righting, before the book could be closed on Brian Dix, was the exhumation of the unfortunate Tammy's body from her unmarked grave. Under a cloak of anonymity courtesy of Warren's influential friends, Brodie was able to divulge the whereabouts of her remains without fear of prosecution. Neil arranged for her to be given a proper send off with her nearest and dearest at her graveside. A modest trust fund was set up by Neil and Warren to provide her children with an education. Last but not least Neil saw to it that she had a decent headstone bearing the words, 'Tamara Stoller, beloved mother, wife and daughter', followed by a short poem chosen by her family.

## Bittersweet Humiliation

After their physical wounds had healed and they were fully fit to travel, Neil, Natasha and family said goodbye to the warm hospitality of the Bateson Ranch and returned home to England to rebuild their shattered lives.

Della passed her doctor's exams with flying colours.

# OTHER TITLES IN THE BITTERSWEET SERIES

## Bittersweet Sacrifice

The seminal book in the 'Bittersweet' series.
Published April 2013
Paperback ISBN Number: 978-0-9576285-8-8
Ebook ISBN Number: 978-0-9576285-9-5

Neil Curland is languishing in an Indian summer heat wave when the worst storm in three hundred years throws the Country into a post-apocalyptic turmoil.

Caught up in his own personal hell, Neil finds himself unceremoniously dumped at the feet of the exotic Natasha. What begins as a labour of lust soon migrates into a deeper, darker erotic attraction, but Natasha comes with a dangerous past which just won't lie down and die!

Fate smiles on Neil Curland in the exotic Natasha, but life can weave a convoluted journey of jealousy, betrayal, kidnap, and violence when love is usurped by lust!

When her deranged ex kidnaps Natasha's child, Neil is forced to re-visit his former life in the armed forces; bringing together a task force with the skills to challenge the Provisional IRA at the height of the 'troubles'.

Obsession and erotic brinkmanship weave a convoluted path between misunderstanding and coincidence. Cruel twists of fate see the couple separated by customs, religion and continents as their lives and loves veer off in opposite directions.

Will they ever see each other again?

What does fate have in store for Neil and Natasha?

Be careful what you wish for!

# OTHER TITLES IN THE BITTERSWEET SERIES

**Bittersweet Retribution**

The third book in the Bittersweet series
Published: November 2015
Paperback ISBN Number: 978-0-9576285-7-1
EBook ISBN Number: 978-0-9576285-6-4


The woman must have been about fifteen years her senior. Standing as she was between the fire escape and the rusty remains of the alley gate, she prevented Natasha's escape.

Dire thoughts were creeping into Natasha's mind, she could feel the darkness closing in on her, she felt the nightmare was about to start all over again.

"Are you Natasha?" the older woman questioned.

"Yes," she replied, her voice sounding remote to her, disconnected.

"Natasha, I'm so sorry to have startled you this way. I must speak with you. It's a matter of life and death. I am Anna Bergkamp. I am the wife of Isa Hashim Al-Kooheji."


Natasha's heart began to slow, the muscles in her neck slowly released the stranglehold they had on her throat, allowing her to breathe, refreshing the oxygen supply to her brain. "You nearly made me pass out!" Nervous laughter overcame her power of speech, leaving her alternately sobbing and retching.

"I am so sorry; it was not my intention to frighten you. We have been looking for you for days. I need to speak with you. We need to talk. It's my husband Isa, he is trying to kill me. I think he may be trying to kill us both!"